HAMPTON
HEIGHTS

HAMPTON HEIGHTS

ONE HARROWING NIGHT IN THE
MOST HAUNTED NEIGHBORHOOD
IN MILWAUKEE, WISCONSIN

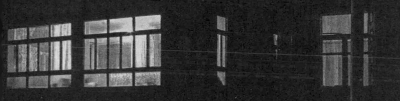

DAN KOIS

HARPER PERENNIAL

NEW YORK • LONDON • TORONTO • SYDNEY • NEW DELHI • AUCKLAND

HARPER PERENNIAL

HarperCollins books may be purchased for educational, business, or sales promotional use. For information, please email the Special Markets Department at SPsales@harpercollins.com.

FIRST EDITION

Designed by Jackie Alvarado

Library of Congress Cataloging-in-Publication Data has been applied for.

ISBN 978-0-06-335875-1

24 25 26 27 28 LBC 5 4 3 2 1

For the Stewarts and the Koises

I remember my own childhood vividly. I knew terrible things, but I knew I mustn't let adults *know* I knew. It would scare them.

—*Maurice Sendak*

HAMPTON HEIGHTS

THE VAN

Later, when they talked about that night, the boys would say that the van must have been cursed.

The van certainly *looked* cursed. It was the species of long white panel van into which, traditionally, perverts lured children. It had no sliding door at the side, only swinging back doors that hung loose on their hinges, ready to fall open at the slightest acceleration. Ten years of hard driving through Wisconsin winters had eaten away at the van's flanks, which were the dark gray of a smoggy sky and pitted with rust the color of dried blood.

The boys knew the van. Early mornings, eating cereal in the warmth of their houses, they heard the roar of the engine, the distant thump of hard rock. The papers were supposed to be there by five, but Kevin, their *Milwaukee Sentinel* delivery manager, always seemed to be a little bit behind. When they peered out their front windows into the predawn gloom, they could just make out Kevin throwing open the back doors and hauling a pile of newspapers to the porch. In the darkness he was a tall silhouette against the taillights. He wore a thin jacket no matter how frigid the weather. His cigarette glowed infernally.

They'd never seen the inside of the van—would never want to.

That van was evil, they said in later years, joking but not joking, when one saw another in a tavern, or when they reconnected on social media. In fact, the van was a miracle, as Kevin could have told them.

It always started, even on the coldest morning. Its engine screamed like a Harley's. It handled like a dream, considering it was basically a shipping container on wheels.

The van wasn't cursed. That wasn't the reason it all went down like that, that night in Hampton Heights.

The boys lived in neighborhoods scattered around the north and east sides, neighborhoods that were their responsibilities, their routes. Each morning when the boys woke to clock radios beeping or buzzing or playing "The Lady in Red" *again* their neighborhoods awaited them. They dressed in the light of bedside lamps, moved quietly through their houses to avoid waking anyone up. After Kevin dropped off the papers, they hauled the stack into the house, a block of newsprint still cold to the touch. They used scissors or a box cutter to snip the dirty yellow plastic cord that bundled them together. Each day's *Sentinel* came in two sections, the front-page section and the rest, so they sat on the floor inserting one part of the paper into the other, sometimes getting distracted by a *Peanuts* or a Bucks photo or, less often, a news story. They checked the drop/add list for changes; they piled the newspapers in their cloth carrier bags; they made their way into the street as dawn began creeping into the sky.

The job made them tired all day at school and dirtied their hands with ink. Adults complained: The paper came too late, the paper came too early, the paper needed to be *between the storm door and the main door*, not just *on the porch* or, worse, *at the end of the driveway*. The job didn't pay well at all. It was just the only job available to a thirteen-year-old who needed money.

But then the flyer appeared one morning, tucked under the yellow cord. Here was a different kind of opportunity.

EXTRA MONEY
FOR HOLIDAYS?

Canvassing Nights
December 14, 15, 16, 17, 18
6:00 PM
Space Limited, Sign Up Now

REMINDER!

All Paper Carriers
Must Canvass Once Per Year

Sell Subscriptions

Get Cash!
Dinner at Burger King!

Burger King! Sigmone Washington's eyes went straight to the bottom of the flyer. Burger King was his favorite restaurant. His mom and dad loved McDonald's, so there he was always eating those sad little beef patties when he could be eating *flame-broiled*. And it was free! Wait—was it free? The flyer didn't exactly say.

Burger King! Ryan Sapp read it again in the porch light. Burger King! His parents disdained fast food, prided themselves on home-cooked meals. Every night at the table, his dad at the head, his mom running and getting everyone more salad, another glass of milk. He'd only ever had Burger King once, at his best friend's birthday party, and it tasted so much better than those home-cooked meals that he would do anything to go there again.

Burger King! Kneeling in the front hallway, Mark Hoglund held the flyer in one hand, rubbed the back of his neck with the other. He could sell newspaper subscriptions. Lay on the charm, tell a few jokes, just like he did with teachers and parents and his church youth group leader. It was harder to be with kids his own age, especially girls; the ease he felt with grown-ups evaporated. But he had to try, because Burger King was where Heather Marchese worked. Heather Marchese who was a high-schooler, Heather Marchese who sat behind him every Sunday in youth group and, every Sunday, doodled on his neck in ballpoint pen.

Burger King! Alessandro Cotrone considered the flyer as he pulled on his coat, tied his scarf. A free dinner already, and cash to boot. How much cash? Probably that depended on how many subscriptions he sold. The question mark at the top of the flyer—EXTRA MONEY FOR HOLIDAYS?—was a tell, he suspected. It would require some real effort to sell those subscriptions, to persuade people to give money to a random kid standing at the door. But he'd done it before.

Burger King! Nishu Shah never got tired of watching the commercials on television: the gleaming patties flipping on a grill in slow motion, the flames flaring up, the vegetables cascading upon the burger in artful disarray. It would kill his parents to know how much their son wanted a hamburger. Before he showed the flyer to his mom, he took a pair of scissors out of the stationery drawer and cut off the last line.

Burger King! Joel Taylor, reading the flyer in his house's cavernous entryway, hoped they would eat first and *then* sell newspapers. A big fast-food meal would generate incredible material for his fart tape.

Now the van was back, idling at the curb on a December evening. Whatever was hidden in its depths, the boys were about to see it.

"Baby," Sigmone's mom called from the living room, "the man's outside waiting for you." He finished tying his shoes and kissed her goodbye. On the wall by the front door, his grandfather smiled from the photo, a young Sigmone grinning on his lap. He picked his way down the icy steps to the ground floor of the duplex.

He usually avoided going out after dark, worried about the knuckleheads just a year or two older who spent the nights getting into trouble, but tonight no one was around. The van idled by the corner of Holton and Concordia. The clouds were fat and blank, illuminated from below by the lights of the strip a block away. It was going to snow tonight, he could tell.

Kevin had a thick mustache, a long brown mullet, and little eyes scrunched into his face. He was drumming on the steering wheel and jumped when he noticed Sigmone waiting outside the passenger door. He reached across to roll down the window. Sigmone had never met Kevin in person, only talked on the phone. He guessed his manager was forty or something.

"Kids in the back, man," Kevin said, pointing over his shoulder. "It's unlocked."

The double doors opened with a groan. Inside it was nearly empty, it turned out. There weren't even any seats behind the driver's row, just the steel floor and the wheel wells on each side. Kevin's hard rock music filled the stale air. Scattered around were loose pages from, Sigmone assumed, centuries of the *Milwaukee Sentinel*.

"You gotta really slam those doors," Kevin called from the front. Even after he pulled the doors shut, Sigmone could still see street light between them, and he sat as far to the front of the truck as he could, his back against the passenger seat, bracing his feet on a wheel well. Somehow, when Kevin accelerated, the doors stayed closed.

Craning his neck, Sigmone could see they were driving north, toward the suburbs. The route was the same as the number 15 bus he took every morning, so Sigmone assumed the other kids they were picking up would be white. He prepared himself for the expressions that would flash across their faces when they opened the doors and saw him.

Ryan saw the van from his window when it pulled up outside his house. His mom joined him. The street was dark enough that they could see themselves reflected clearly, their near-identical faces, his eyes still well below hers.

"You'll be careful?" his mom asked.

"It's fine," he said, zipping his coat.

"I wonder where the other boys will be from," she said.

"They're just other paperboys," he said. "We're not gonna be life-long friends." He saw her carefully not respond, saw her reach out for a hug. He squirmed away. They must have been lit up like a movie screen in the window.

On his way down the sidewalk, the salt his dad had made him scatter in anticipation of snow crunched under his feet. Kevin gestured toward the back, and when Ryan wrenched the doors open, he revealed a lone black kid sitting on the floor. The kid was big, way bigger than Ryan, but he looked so miserable wedged up against the passenger seat that Ryan could hardly be intimidated. Though he hardly ever talked to the few black kids at his school, he managed to squawk out a "Hey."

The boy nodded. Ryan closed the doors, opened them, tried closing them again. He said, "Are these, like, actually—aahhh!" For that was the moment when Kevin hit the gas. Ryan tumbled into the doors, which gave, sickeningly, just an inch—but held. He shrieked, he knew, the noise that always made his dad wince.

The black kid was kind enough to pretend not to notice the sound. "I thought you were going out" was all he said.

"Oh my God," Ryan said, scrambling forward as the van bumped along the road. "Oh my *God*."

Mark was watching TV in the family room when he heard the horn. He checked himself in the foyer mirror: his Ocean Pacific sweatshirt, his freshly cut hair. "Yeah, make sure you look good," his brother said from the top of the stairs. "For when he molests you."

"Shut up, dick." Danny had been a paperboy, too, when he was Mark's age. He'd gone out canvassing, come back rolling his eyes. It was impossible to sell subscriptions, Kevin was a creep, and so on. Mark was pretty sure the problem was that Danny was a dick. In a moment of weakness, he had once asked Danny if he thought Heather Marchese liked him. "No," Danny had said. "You're a shithead." Now Danny worked at Kopp's Custard, where every time Mark showed up Danny pretended not to know him.

But it had to mean something, right? Heather Marchese was funny and cute and she always sat in the chair behind him, every Sunday. And every Sunday he felt the cold tip of her ballpoint on his neck. After the first time it happened, he recalled, he'd spent five minutes in the bathroom at home, angling his mom's hand mirror, trying to get a glimpse of what she'd written. He was afraid it was something mean, KICK ME or something, but when he finally caught the image, he saw she'd drawn a delicate vine creeping up his neck, a flower sprouting from its top. The thought of talking to her at Burger King made him feel sick, but he also couldn't wait.

The horn blared again. Mark flipped his brother off and ran out the door, pulling on his coat as he went. There were two other kids in the back of the van: a tall black kid and a short, chubby boy with freckles. "Sorry it's so cold back there," Kevin said as he threw the van in gear. "Heater's on the fritz." Neither of the kids was talking, and Mark always felt like it was his job to get people talking, so he said, "I'm Mark. Who are you guys?"

They were Ryan and Sigmone. On the way to the next house, Mark and Ryan talked about Weird Al Yankovic.

Al had considered asking Kevin to get picked up somewhere else, Food Lane maybe, so the other kids wouldn't see him coming out of his town house. When kids at school learned he lived here, they put on an apologetic facial expression, as if they'd learned he had a childhood disease. The town house was perfectly nice, his mom told him, and he knew she was right, but that didn't stop him from feeling bad when he saw the kinds of houses his classmates lived in.

But as he approached the van, he saw that all the other kids must be in the windowless back, from which loud noises emanated. When he opened the doors, he revealed two boys singing at the tops of their lungs. "Dare to be stupid!" they shouted, laughing. A black kid watched them warily. None of them, he realized, could see the town house, none of them even cared about where he lived. *No one is thinking about you as much as you think they are*, his mom had told him once.

One of the boys asked Al his name, then cheered when he said it. "Weird Al!" they shouted. Al felt his face heat up as he clambered into the van, but he'd take it. He pushed himself against the wall and nodded at the black kid, whose name was Sigmone. The other white kids, Mark and Ryan, went on singing. If he listened carefully, maybe he could learn the words.

Nishu's mom didn't want him to go. "He'll be too frightened," she said. His dad was exasperated, he could tell, but was trying not to show it. Instead he reminisced about all the weird jobs he'd worked when he was young: valet, fisher, assistant in his uncle's shipping office. Most of the time Nishu felt no desire to go to India, but the idea of a country that would let a kid do all that made him laugh. Here all he was allowed to do was deliver newspapers.

"Don't you remember the movie?" his mom asked. They had all gone to *E.T.* together, and Nishu, scared of the doctors in the astronaut suits, had hid under his chair. That was five years ago.

"That was five years ago!" his dad said.

"We don't even know this *Milwaukee Sentinel* person," she said.

The van pulled up and Nishu grabbed his backpack. "I have my homework," he said, "we'll be done at nine," and charged out the door.

In fact, his mom had met Kevin before, when she demanded to interrogate him before she would let Nishu start delivering papers. (She said he seemed like an idiot.) That had been embarrassing, but not as embarrassing as his mom now shouting out the front door, "Buckle your seat belt, Nishu!"

Kevin tried to wave Nishu to the back but Nishu stood miserably at the passenger window. Kevin rolled it down and smoke billowed from the van. "Can I sit here?" Nishu asked.

"Is he *smoking*?" his mom called.

"Sorry," Nishu added.

Kevin flicked his cigarette out the window, past Nishu's ear, and waved cheerily to Nishu's mom. "Sure, yeah man, no problem," he said. "Just move that shit down there."

The seat was covered with notebooks and pens and clipboards and—oh, wow, this was a big knife. Nishu piled them all up and placed them on the grimy floor of the van, then set the knife, tucked in some kind of scabbard, atop the pile. Then he put his backpack on top of the knife. Even when he buckled up, his mom wouldn't leave the front door. Finally Nishu muttered, "Just drive, please," and Kevin peeled out with a sound he knew his mom would talk about for weeks, maybe years.

At the sixth and final house, Kevin had to pull up to a gate, roll down the window, and announce himself to an intercom. From the intercom came a squawk. In the front seat, Nishu said, "A kid *lives* here?" He turned to address the four boys in the back: "You gotta see this. It's like a castle." The other boys shoved the back doors open and clambered out to behold: It was a castle. A long driveway led from the gate to a massive cream-colored mansion, as big as a movie theater. Floodlights on either side of bright red double doors picked out the half-dozen columns reaching to the roof.

"Is this . . . Lake Drive?" Al asked. Everyone knew Lake Drive was where the mansions were.

"I think so," said Nishu.

One of the doors opened and a figure in a blue coat hurried out. Lit now by the floodlights like a burglar caught by the police, the figure stopped, went back into the house, and in a moment reappeared carrying a big green backpack. The boys stood in silence for the long minute it took the kid to trudge down the driveway. He pushed the gate open and stepped through. The gate closed behind him with a gentle clang. As if coming out of a trance, the other boys returned to the van and climbed in.

Joel entered last. He hoisted his backpack over the transom, placing it carefully on the steel floor, then climbed in and closed the doors. Then he opened the doors and closed them again, because they didn't seem that closed. As the van began to move, Joel set the backpack between his knees and unzipped it, revealing the biggest boom box any of them had ever seen. Huge woofers. A CD player. A *graphic equalizer*. Joel set the boom box on the floor of the van, then pulled out a microphone.

"Are we on *Star Search*?" Sigmone asked.

Joel tried to untangle the hopelessly knotted microphone cord. "This is great," he said. "I don't have any black farts on my tape at all."

Everyone burst into shocked giggles, even Sigmone. Joel hit eject on the boom box and pulled out a cassette tape. He held it up under the dome light. On its label was written, in blue pen, FART TAPE.

"Fart tape," Mark said, unnecessarily, with wonder in his voice.

"I've been working on it since the summer," Joel said. He was skinny, almost as tall as Sigmone, with a blond crew cut. "It's mostly me, but some of my friends are on it, too."

He slid the tape back into the cassette deck, rewound a moment, and hit play. The boys crowded close to the blessed object, to hear over the noise of the van. Nishu's entire top half was hanging over the back of the seat. Someone on the tape was saying "Here, here," and then there was a rustling, and then a pause, and then a loud honking fart. Then laughter, on the tape, in the van. They couldn't help it.

"How many farts do you have?" Sigmone asked.

"I'm almost done with Side A."

"You have *forty-five minutes* of farts on that tape," Mark said.

"Thirty minutes. It's a sixty-minute tape. I got a lot at Boy Scout camp."

Everyone nodded. It was amazing. There was no other word for it. They discussed its amazingness for a while, and then Al said, "Oh, I've got one. I've got one!"

"Get him the mike!" said Nishu, waving frantically from the front seat. By now Joel had untangled the cord. He directed Al to put the microphone directly under his butt, then hit record just before Al let loose. All six of the kids lost it.

"Oh God, it *reeks*," Ryan said.

"Smells like a hodag," said Mark.

"A *what*?"

"Like, a monster from the north woods," Joel said. He'd learned about them during that mostly miserable Boy Scout camp weekend.

"Hodags are, like, made of dead cows," Al said. "How dare you say my farts smell that bad."

"Worse!" said Sigmone, and they all cracked up again.

The van crunched to a halt. Kevin turned to face them. "I swear to God," he said. "You idiots having a good time?"

"Yes," said Ryan.

"We're here."

"Where are we?" asked Mark.

"We're in Hampton Heights."

One by one they climbed from the van and stood on the pavement, hands in pockets. No one would have said aloud that the neighborhood was spooky, but it was spooky. They were standing in the parking lot of a tavern called Hampton House, and the lights of the bar gleamed in the fog. From inside came the murmur of music. Clouds obscured the moon. Half the streetlights were burned out.

"That's Hampton there," Sigmone said, pointing at the street sign. They knew Hampton. It went all the way east to the lake, through the parts of town where they all went to school. In those neighborhoods, the houses were nicer. Here they were small and wooden, one story, with little detached garages set at the tops of the buckling driveways.

Ryan, looking at the street sign, made a noise of surprise. "There's a 54th Street?"

"There's a every number street," Sigmone said.

"My grandma lives on 83rd Street," said Al.

"Good for your grandma," said Joel, looking around to confirm the sickness of his burn. Al just shook his head.

Kevin, meanwhile, was pulling a sheaf of papers from under the passenger seat and smoothing them out. Nishu had stepped all over them. "Marching orders," he said. "I'm splitting you up. You and you, you're already getting along. You're a pair." Mark and Ryan high-fived. He paired Sigmone and Joel, Nishu and Al, and handed a clipboard to each duo. "Anyone ever done this before?" he asked.

"My brother did," said Mark.

Joel perked up. "Good for—"

"Man, shut up," Sigmone said.

Kevin eyed Mark. "Danny, is that right? He didn't sell shit, in my memory."

"Probably not."

"Sort of a dick."

"For sure."

"Well, you can do better than him." Kevin pulled a smoke from a pack in his shirt pocket, found a lighter, shielded the cigarette from the wind. The boys paged through the printouts on the clipboards, trying to make sense of them. Kevin puffed. "Those are master lists of everyone in the neighborhood who is *not* a subscriber," he said. "Your job is to go house to house, door to door, and sell subscriptions to these people."

"How much does it cost?" Al asked. He already had his printout pinned neatly under the clipboard's steel clasp.

"Ten bucks for three months. But push the year, it's a good deal— twenty-five for the year. Plus if you do the year you get a commemorive"— he stopped himself—"a commemora-tive plate."

"What does it co-mmem-o-rate?" Ryan asked.

"I dunno," Kevin said. "Probably the Packers." He took a pull off the cigarette, and the smoke faded into the fog. "We can send them a bill. Or if they want they can pay now. Don't let 'em write a check. Cash only."

"Where's Fairmount?" Al asked, angling his list toward the one streetlight.

"North," said Kevin, pointing across Hampton. "About a block that way. Whoever sells the most subscriptions," he added, "gets twenty bucks." That got their attention. "Meet back here at the van at eight thirty. And don't be late, or no one gets Burger King." Sigmone raised his hand and Kevin said, "What."

"I don't have a watch."

"So ask someone the time. Figure it out."

"I've got a watch," Joel said, and brandished it. To Kevin he added, "Can you lock the doors? My boom box is in there."

Kevin looked at Nishu. "You?" But Nishu kept his backpack on. Kevin made a big show of locking the back, then tucked the keys in the wheel well. "Okay," he said—here came the big pep talk—"go make some money."

Ryan and Mark headed south. Sigmone and Joel turned west. Nishu and Al crossed Hampton to the north. Kevin waited a moment, then tossed his cigarette butt to the ground, where it hissed in a patch of dirty snow. Before the bartender at Hampton House could even say hello, Kevin had ordered his first beer.

KEVIN

If it wasn't for Theresa treating him like that, Kevin Kaczorowski never even would've looked at the woman in the bar.

The bartender was taking his sweet time pulling Kevin's second beer. That was the way it was when you were the new guy in a neighborhood tavern. He'd been the new guy in plenty, driving kids all over the city to sell newspapers. Sometimes the bar he ended up at was lively, exciting, like sometimes the neighborhoods were lively, exciting. And sometimes he was in Hampton Heights, where no one he knew lived and where the tavern was a weird mix: black and white, old and young, everyone seeming to recognize one another but also staking out their own space.

Down at the end of the bar, the tender wiped the counter with a towel like a bartender in a TV show, talking to an older blonde in a Packers jersey. She nodded and laughed at something the bartender said, then looked down Kevin's way. Kevin had been waving his cardboard coaster to get the guy's attention, but shifted the move—smoothly, he thought—into a greeting to the blonde. She lifted her cocktail. Her long earrings sparkled in the beerlight. Even from here he could see how long her nails were.

He stood the coaster on its edge, flipped it back onto the bar. There was basically nothing to look at in this tavern, which resembled every other tavern in the city. A single room, square, lit by neon beer signs. Low ceilings to keep things warm. Wood-paneled walls covered in Packers and Badgers schedules. The TV was showing some cheesy horror movie, a shapeshifting monster taking men apart. A sign on the wall, above the liquor, caught his eye.

Our Credit Manager
Is Helen Waite
If You Want Credit
Go to Helen Waite

What a weird thing to put on a sign. Why would a shitty bar like this even have a credit manager?

"You need another one?" The bartender had finally sauntered over and noticed Kevin's empty glass.

"You bet," Kevin said. Did he ever. Theresa was sleeping with Crazy TV Barry again.

She said that Barry wasn't like he was in his TV commercials. "He's just a normal guy," she said. A normal guy Kevin was sure she'd slept with last year, during their fight. A normal guy Theresa still called sometimes, just coincidentally when they weren't getting along. A normal guy who drove an Audi. What normal guy drove an Audi?

In his commercials, for the big appliance store out on Brown Deer Road, Crazy TV Barry ranted and raved, a nonstop stream of come-ons and shrieks and gobbling noises. Everyone told him he was CRAZY to cut prices this low! He wielded a giant pair of scissors to slice big cartoony price tags in half. His competitors despaired! His customers celebrated! Sometimes the guys in white coats hauled him away to a padded room, but that's what it takes to offer low, low prices on Amana freezers. His commercials appeared so frequently—between innings of Brewers games, during time-outs in Packers games, sometimes two or three commercials in a row during the late movie on Channel 18—that Kevin, like everyone he knew, had parts of his patter memorized. "They said I was *nuts* when I asked, *what's lower than zero percent financing?!*" Even Crazy TV Barry's phone number was as familiar to Kevin as his own: 466-1987. Last year it had been 466-1986. He imagined Crazy TV Barry, eyes bugging out, haranguing some poor asshole at the phone company to secure the numbers in advance. "Whaddya mean you don't have 1996? You gotta have 1996!"

Kevin knew that Crazy TV Barry drove an Audi because this afternoon, parked kitty-corner from Theresa's duplex, he'd watched Crazy TV Barry pull up in an Audi, deep blue and sleek as hell. He'd watched Theresa clip-clop out of her house in heels, smiling and waving at the car. She'd looked happy, at ease. Kevin tried to remember the last time she'd looked that happy to see him. When she got in the Audi, she hugged the entirely recognizable driver. His hair was combed and he wore a suit, not a straitjacket, but it was definitely him. His license plate read CRZYBRY.

He'd waited until they pulled away, then driven home, glumly flipping from ballad to ballad on the radio. It was true that things hadn't been great. When they first got together, five years ago now—Jesus!—he was twenty-one and they went out all the time, drinking with buddies or to the bowling alley or just driving. He had money because he had a job, one that at twenty-one had seemed amazing—someone paying him just to drive newspapers around? Now she worked a lot of nights at Froedtert Hospital, so she came home tired and they were always renting a video or talking about her fucked-up family. Sometimes they had sex, depending on whether she fell asleep during the movie. His job, once a stepping stone to something else, was now just what he did. He started work at four in the morning, but he still wanted to have some fun.

But if she was so tired, what was she doing going out tonight? She had a midnight-to-eight in post-op. But there she was, dressed for dinner, more decked out than he'd seen her in a long time. When they watched movies at her place, she wore pajamas and put her hair up and they'd eat on the couch, some green salad or pesto pasta—she was on a health food kick so she hardly ever cooked burgers anymore.

When he'd finally gotten home, he'd turned the van off and then simply sat in silence. The only sound was the wind blowing outside. The forecast was for snow. In the mirror, his eyes were red. What did Crazy TV Barry have that he didn't have? Money? A nice car? Fancy suits? Celebrity? A successful business? The list continued; he didn't need to go on. But he'd loved Theresa for so long. He couldn't believe she was going to dump him for a guy who appeared on TV foaming at the mouth.

When he finally snapped out of it he went inside, ate a can of ravioli. She was probably dining on steak downtown. After his shower he stood naked in the bedroom, pawing through the underwear drawer. On his dresser sat the Hampton Heights master list he'd pulled from the giant printer at work. It was slim pickings, probably, a neighborhood without too much extra money to spend. He was well behind his quota, hopelessly behind for the year, probably. Well, what was the paper gonna do? It wasn't like there were people lining up to take this job. Were there?

Kevin was completely out of clean underwear. In the depths of his closet, he recalled, he had a pair of flannel boxers Theresa had given him for his birthday in July. "They're warm," she'd said. "You'll love them this winter." He pulled the boxers out of the gift bag and tore off the tags. They were soft and plaid, navy blue and black. They did look warm, he had to admit. He wasn't really a boxers guy, liked his shit a little more secure, but it was gonna be a cold one tonight. He pulled them on, brushed a few pieces of navy blue fuzz out of his leg hairs, then got dressed.

Now at the bar, he felt those boxers bunching up as he shifted on his stool, trying to get comfortable. They were warm, but in the overheated tavern they were too much. He had to keep surreptitiously pulling them down through his jeans. A third beer got the bartender to deign, finally, to engage in some conversation. He thought Randy White was the answer at QB; Kevin argued in favor of the new kid, Majkowski. "We finally got a chance to put a Pole in charge," he said. People loved Randy White, all out of keeping with his actual skill level, just because he used to be the Badgers' quarterback. This was nuts, he explained to the bartender. Just because you were the star on the mediocre Wisconsin college team does not mean you deserved to start for the Wisconsin professional team! There are other quarterbacks out there!

"I gotta take some orders," the guy finally said, which was maybe true. The tavern was filling up. "But you should talk to Laurie down there." He gestured down the bar to the blonde with the jersey, who was digging through her purse. "She can argue about the Packers forever."

"Oh yeah?" said Kevin. Talking to a random chick at a random bar had not really occurred to him. In fact, he'd never picked up a woman in a bar, never even tried to. He knew he should approach her, should start talking to her, but he felt honestly exhausted by the idea of starting at zero with a whole nother woman. She would have so many things to say! She would have so many problems she'd want to unload on him! He directed his attention to the TV instead, only to see the movie fade out and Crazy TV Barry appear. He was dangling upside down from some kind of winch, unshaven, shouting about how Santa Claus was going to spring him in time for National TV and Appliance's Pre-Christmas Madhouse.

"You know what?" he said to the bartender. "Tell her the next one's on me."

He'd never tried to pick up a woman in a bar because he'd been so loyal for so long. He'd met Theresa on his twenty-first birthday, when his old high school coach had brought her along to drinks. She was Coach's neighbor, a year older than Kevin, in nursing school. "I've known her since she was just a little thing!" Coach had said, and he'd liked the way she laughed, full of affection for the guy. He remembered walking with her after last call that night, not wasted but buzzed. It must have been warm—it was July. He made a joke about growing up next to Coach and she rolled her eyes, probably said something funny, she was always joking about Coach's wandering eyes. They ended up at some elementary school in Tosa, sitting on the swings like little kids. Just talking. He barely remembered anything she'd said, he was so wrapped up in the feeling. Discovery. Like he was Indiana Jones and every new moment opened up a fresh room full of treasures.

Well, he thought bitterly. Everyone knew what happened once Indy got his hands on the treasure. Here came the giant rolling rock.

The blonde at the end of the bar had accepted her drink, and she raised it to him with a nod. He shifted uncomfortably on his stool as he nodded back. Theresa's fucking boxer shorts! They reminded him of her every time he moved. Maybe he should go to the john and fix them, or even just take them off and go commando. He was just buzzed enough to chuckle at that idea. He had to piss anyway.

But just as he was about to stand she got up, the blonde. She didn't approach him but walked to the far corner of the room, to the jukebox, a surprisingly fancy model considering it didn't seem to get much use. (So far, all there'd been to listen to was boring oldies from behind the bar and the screams of men from the TV.) As she leaned up against the machine, pressing buttons to flip through the records, he had the opportunity to really check her out.

Her hair cascaded from her feather bangs down over her shoulders, obscuring the name on her home jersey. Number fifteen: Bart Starr. Her jeans were tight in the back, looking good, and she wore low heels, nothing dramatic like Theresa. She was short, but there was a lot in that little package. She had the kind of tan you didn't see that often in December.

She plugged a quarter in, pushed some buttons. To Kevin's disappointment, her song started slow and keyboardy. Why would you make a whole big show of your walk over to the jukebox, then pick a song this boring? Just some guy bitching over synthesizers about praying for strength or something.

But oh, then the drums kicked in.

And oh! the guitars rang out. And oh! the singer made up his mind. He wasn't wasting no more time!

Here I go again on my own
Goin' down the only road I've ever known

Kevin was slapping his legs to the beat, nodding his head. He lifted his beer in tribute to the woman who'd picked this fucking incredible song and she, leaning against the jukebox, pumped a fist in response. There was something electric in her eyes. A glint he could see from here. The whole tavern was singing now, a dozen people or more, all these people who hadn't cared a bit about one another before, united by this song, and the bartender drummed on the counter furiously. On the final chorus, as the tavern clapped along, Kevin found he had tears in his eyes. And now he was standing at the pay phone, receiver at his ear, listening to the ring through the line. Like a drifter, he was born to walk alone.

To his surprise, Theresa answered. "It's me," he said. The bar was quieter now, a different song playing, but he still felt the pulse, the power, of the song in his heart.

"Where are you?" she asked. "I thought you were canvassing tonight."

"The kids are out. I'm waiting for them to be done." At the bar, the blonde was high-fiving everyone in sight. "We need to break up."

He could hear the TV in her living room. Tony Danza's voice. She must be watching *Who's the Boss?* He was about to ask if she'd heard him when she said, "Why are you telling me this now? Don't you have to pick up the kids soon?"

He turned to face the wall of the bar. What did she mean, why now? And why didn't she sound surprised, or upset? She sounded like she was appraising him—like she'd suddenly seen something in him and was curious to know more.

"Why now is because what were you doing tonight?"

"I went out with Barry tonight."

He spluttered. He punched the wall. The bartender was giving him the look of death. "I *know* you went out with Barry!"

"I know you know, because I saw your fucking van when he picked me up."

"Did you sleep with him?"

She made a noise of exhaustion. Her! How dare she! "A, it's none of your business. B, no, I didn't happen to sleep with him tonight."

"Yeah, right."

"It is right. It is right." Theresa had maintained, for a year now, that Barry had always been a perfect gentleman, that they were just friends. He liked going to the symphony which, news to Kevin, she said she did, too.

"Why him?" Kevin asked, then immediately remembered all the reasons he'd previously come up with. "Don't answer that. I have been loyal to you for five years!"

"Ugh," she said. "Loyalty."

"And what does that mean?" He was covering the phone with his hand now, trying not to appear to everyone in the bar as if he was arguing with his girlfriend.

"I'm loyal, too, and what do I get for it? You giving me shit all the time. You not taking my job seriously. You call it loyalty. I call it punishment."

"What are you talking about?"

"Kevin, what do you think *I* need?"

Kevin laughed, or rather, he simply said "Ha." "What you *need* is to come to your senses and realize—"

"Forget it," she said. "You never listen."

"Oh, I heard you," he said. "You're making excuses for cheating when you—"

"I *didn't even cheat on you yet*," she hissed. He sat down heavily on the wobbly stool that lived by the pay phone, had lived there since cavemen first fashioned it from primordial trees. "Of *course* I want to sleep with Barry!" she continued. "But I've been waiting for you to give me a reason not to." She snorted. "What a dumbass I am."

"But," he said, but nothing.

"I gotta go to work and deal with patients all night," she said, finally. "I would love for us to talk, really talk, at a reasonable time and place. You drunk in a bar is not reasonable."

"I'm not drunk yet," he said, but she'd already hung up. He placed the phone on its hook and slowly turned around on the stool, feeling like everyone in the bar had heard not only his side of the conversation but also, somehow, hers. But no one was even looking at him.

Except the blonde. She smiled.

He stood up. This was stupid. It was stupid for him to feel so bad. He'd spent his prime years dating the same woman, he'd stuck by her even as she became a boring *nurse*, a nurse who likes the *symphony*, and this was how she treated him? And then he was standing next to the blonde, but he hadn't figured out what to say. He settled on "Hey."

"Hey there," she said. She gestured to the stool next to her. "Heavy conversation?"

"It was nobody," he said.

She smiled brilliantly and looked him right in the eye. He felt suddenly like he'd had the air knocked out of him, that's how hot she looked. "That's good," she breathed.

He was Kevin. She was Laurie. He complimented her Bart Starr jersey. "What a player," she said.

"A leader," he agreed, flagging down another beer from the bartender. "I don't really remember the glory days. You and me, we were too young for those."

She laughed tolerantly, confirming his belief that she was older than him, maybe even in her thirties. "You're hilarious," she said.

"You know, everyone wears their Packers shit but it's never, like, Eddie Lee Ivery. It's never someone from now. It's always the guys from way back."

"We had legends walking among us. Now they're just"—she wrinkled her nose—"men."

"I thought about trying out this year, during the strike, but I didn't want to be a scab." In October all the NFL teams had replaced their rosters with nonunion players for three games. The Scab Packers had won two of them. "A lot of the guys I played with went to the tryouts and said I would've had a chance."

"Oh yeah?" She gave him a once-over, like a scout. It had a frank sexual air that thrilled him. "What position?"

"I was a safety."

"Quarterback of the defense."

"You know your shit."

"I've watched football for a *long* time," she said.

It was true: At safety he'd had to call the plays, keep guys organized, be a leader of men. After Tosa, Kevin had done two years at Stevens Point but got kicked off the team by the has-been coach. His buddy Travis, who'd played at UW, had made it to final cuts at the scab tryouts, but told him that most of the players there had some NFL experience, even if it was just a couple of training camps. They weren't really plumbers and weightlifters, the way the news made it out.

"Those teams in the '60s, they were something to see," Laurie said. Her nails curled around her glass, and her face shifted into a smile. "My last boyfriend had a tattoo across his back." She reached toward Kevin and his breath caught, but she merely turned him by the shoulder so she could touch a path across his back, five touches for five letters. "G R E G G, like on his jersey. The damnedest thing."

"Wow."

"Yeah. And now Forrest Gregg's the coach and they suck and that tattoo is embarrassing."

"To permanent devotion," he said, raising his glass.

"I haven't seen you around here," she said after she sipped. "You new to Hampton Heights?" She leaned in to hear what he had to say. Her eyes were deep, brown, rimmed with red. She was smiling. Her teeth were bright.

"Just here for the night." He explained about his job, tried to make it sound more managerial and less like babysitting. "I'm killing time while they're out canvassing."

Her smile got wider somehow. "You brought a bunch of cute little paperboys here?" she said. "The old ladies are gonna eat 'em up."

"Well, the elderly tend to already be subscribers."

"There's families been here for a century or more," Laurie said. She pulled a maraschino from her old fashioned, set it on a napkin, and speared it with a fingernail. "Nights like this, when the mist comes off the creek, you might as well be in a village in Bavaria."

"So you're saying they're not gonna sell a lot."

"There are some newer families, in from the city. They might be interested in your boys."

"Sounds sorta dirty when you say it like that."

She shrugged and brought the red, red cherry to her red, red mouth. "I'm not interested in boys," she said. "I'm interested in men."

They each did a shot and then left so fast he mistook the black looks the other men in the bar gave him for jealousy. He didn't even see the bartender pick up the twenty Laurie had left under her coaster.

Out in the cold, shocking after so long spent in that hotbox. He didn't feel normal. He felt gloriously out of his head. He was taking advantage of the moment, or the moment was taking advantage of him. He was glad he didn't see any of his carriers as he stumbled, giggling, after her. He checked his watch: still half an hour before he had to meet them back at the van. By the time he won the battle with the zipper of his coat, they'd arrived at her house.

She lived on the right half of a side-by-side. He stared at the door, at its knocker, ornately carved in the shape of a tree. He could stare at the knocker forever and find new details: the intricate leaves, the roughness of the bark. The hole in the trunk where creatures lived, into which he felt himself falling. Around him the traffic on Hampton echoed; the jingle of her keys sounded like sleigh bells. Somewhere, far away, wolves howled. Down, down, into the trunk he went. It was safe here, and dark, and all around him was the living tree, ancient and implacable. All around him sprouted the most beautiful blue flowers, tiny and brave against the winter's chill. Each had four skinny petals that unfurled and beckoned him forward like fingers. He could smell them, bright and clear. He could reach out and touch them. But—

The tree was gone. She had opened the door and swung it away. He couldn't believe how cold he was now, every part of his body freezing except under those flannel boxers, so when she beckoned him in, he followed. Inside it was hot, almost steaming, and something smelled delicious: a sharp, herbal scent, with a lingering rusty note, like his grandma's house when she'd been frying steaks. His nose was up in the air like a beast's, he realized, but she only laughed. "You hungry?" she asked. "I bet you are. I've been cooking."

Was he hungry? That can of ravioli had been a long time ago. And as the warmth returned to his limbs, he felt ravenous, like he could eat anything you put in front of him. "We just made some lapskaus," she said. "Come on in." The kitchen was the first room in the house, just past the front hall, cozy and narrow, a rope of garlic hanging on the wall and a big pot burbling on the stove. She pulled out a Zippo and set it to a trio of candles on the counter. Lapskaus, he dimly recalled, was some kind of Scandy stew. "Norwegian," she confirmed when he asked. "Been simmering all day."

"You're Norwegian?" He looked around for someplace to put his coat, now that he was in the sauna of the tiny kitchen, and, failing to find a good place for it, held it over his arm.

"Going way back. But I've been here a long time." She winked and delivered a joke she'd made before: "Don't ask me how long." He laughed dutifully. How old *was* she? She was definitely a hot older lady, but he couldn't nail it down. From different angles and in different light she changed; in the bar she'd seemed like she could even be in her forties. But here, in the flickering candles, her face looked smoother, though her voice was still raspy and sexy. She was so little! She even had to reach up to ladle the stew from the tall stockpot into a bowl, the muscles working under her browned upper arms. He wasn't that tall of a guy, but he towered over her. He imagined what it'd be like to pick her up, to move her from one place to another. He knocked his head gently against a pot hanging from a hook. The pot clanked against others, a clattering chorus.

His mom would be disappointed in his manners. He devoured the stew, hunched over the kitchen counter, but he felt as though he hadn't eaten in days. He stared into the bowl, the slick of fat on the broth's surface, iridescent, ever moving. It spread across the bowl like a thunderstorm filling the sky. Inside the bowl there were secrets, and he felt himself diving down, down.

He blinked. He'd finished his stew. He felt faintly embarrassed, but it was clear Laurie didn't stand on ceremony. "I love to watch a hungry man eat," she said, opening Miller Lites for them.

"So how long have you lived here?" he asked, trying to keep it normal.

Maybe that was the wrong question, because she screwed up her face in disgust and took a long pull from the beer. "Ugh, forever," she said. "Way too long." But then she kept talking. She lived with her sister—"She's in her bedroom in the back"—and had been here with her for years, kind of supported her. The way she glided over it, Kevin suspected some kind of disability. Laurie worked as a travel agent, specializing in Scandinavia. "Beautiful place. Anyway, I sell package tours, old people visiting the Old Country one last time."

"I bet you're good at it," Kevin said. "I know about sales."

"I'm sort of the weird one in the office." She reached up and ran a nail along the rope of garlic. "A lot of these girls, they've settled down, settled in."

"Not you."

"I always want something *new*. They think I'm a bitch because I can't stand their boring husbands. They should be glad I don't set my sights on those boys, because they wouldn't stand a chance, right?" Kevin nodded with one hundred percent sincerity, and she laughed delightedly. "That's right. You know."

"So if you're not settling down . . ."

"I'm gonna *travel*, Kevin. Get out of Milwaukee. Get away from—" She gestured around her, *everything*, but it was clear that what she wanted to say was *my sister*. "I've almost got it all set up. Wherever I go,

I'm gonna be a whole nother person. Like a butterfly. I'm going to shed my skin and spread my wings and just fly."

"That's amazing," said Kevin, though he didn't think that was how butterflies worked. Wasn't there a whole thing with a chrysalis? "You want to be a different person."

She put a hand on his arm. "I've spent my whole life being what I'm supposed to be. I want to be me." She grimaced as if she'd revealed too much. Probably she worried that he was so perceptive he'd see right through her, suss out her secrets. He felt it polite to move on.

"I'm not a big travel guy, myself," he said. "I went to Chicago once with some buddies, but we got so lost we bailed and drove home before someone killed us."

"A homebody."

"I guess. It's just—my friends are here. My girlfriend's here." She raised an eyebrow. "My ex. We just broke up. Today, actually."

"Oh, honey." His chest tingled where she laid her hand on it. And then she was in a different place, by the door at the end of the kitchen, and she said, "Follow me."

Wasn't that the door to the front hall? No: It led deeper into the house, into a living room as warm and alive as a greenhouse. There were houseplants everywhere along the walls, growing from deep corners, vines erupting from pots, leaves fluttering in an unfelt breeze. There didn't seem to be windows, so he wondered how she even kept them alive. Must be magic. Here the scent was piney and peppery. "Are those, like, juniper candles?" he asked of the flickering lights, and when he turned she was so close to him, looking up into his eyes. She breathed deeply and kissed the corner of his mouth. Then she walked away toward the stereo.

Well, in a cartoon, he'd have squeezed his can of beer so hard it spurted all over the place, but this was real life, no matter how much it was starting to resemble every *Penthouse Forum* he'd ever read. *I never thought I'd be writing in with a story like this*, he thought, grinning. He couldn't stop grinning. He took one glug of the beer, two, three, set it down on the coffee table.

He had to pee, was the problem, but there was no way he was interrupting this story for something that stupid. He would just hold it. Chugging the beer had not been a good idea, actually. While she dropped a CD into the tray and tapped it closed, he laid his coat on the back of the couch and then unbunched his stupid boxers, which were gathering all up in his butt. Then he held his hands before his face and watched them flicker and shimmy in the candlelight. The shadows moving across them held a message, if only he could read it.

Don Henley was playing. Laurie sat on the couch and beckoned him forward. Now that he was moving, the room seemed so big, like a cavern. It seemed impossible he would ever reach her—it was so many steps, and each step required such concentration: lift the foot, throw it forward, plant it, repeat. It was with a real sense of accomplishment that he arrived, finally, at the couch, and settled himself next to her.

"So what about you?" he asked. "Your boyfriend Forrest Gregg still in the picture?"

She shook her head. "It was too much. My sister and all."

"Family's hard."

"Yes!" she replied, so ardently that he wondered if he'd said something accidentally profound. "They have this hold on you, and it takes so much to break free."

Kevin, who felt no particular obligation to his parents—he went home for supper with them once a month or so, and that was fine—nonetheless nodded understandingly.

"Sometimes you just have to make sacrifices for the people you love."

"Totally," he said. At that she gave him a glance, and he worried he'd sounded too stupid, so he added, "At least you know what's the most important, for you."

"I guess," she said. "It's just—" She looked away and let a silence linger, Don Henley crooning in the background, the plants swaying to the music. He didn't know what to say, so he was grateful when she picked back up. "I'm so close to getting out. I've been so close." She looked back at him. "I know it's going to happen soon."

"Cheers to that." He raised his hand, which did not have a beer in it. She looked down at the table and slipped a coaster under his can. "I wish I was like that," he continued. "You know—confident. Comfortable in my own skin."

She traced a fingernail along his bicep. "Nice skin," she said. Her interest in him was intoxicating, although he supposed that could just be the beer. She leaned close and breathed in. He felt himself pulled closer to her from deep inside. She touched his collar with her hand, unbuttoned his top button, and slid a finger between his undershirt and his skin so it rested just on his collarbone. He could feel it there, thrumming with his pulse, the nail sharp on his skin but not hurting him, just resting, waiting for whatever the next thing would be.

The next thing was a kiss. It lasted so long that Kevin's attention started on his own breath—surely beer and stew and Marlboro Lights—but then had time to move elsewhere, to how much he needed to piss, to the plants in the corners and the candles flickering the smell of gin into the air, her fingernail at his neck, her tongue coaxing its way alongside his, exploring his mouth, and it was as if it were filling him up, drawing his very breath out, and the sensation was so surprising and wonderful that he pulled away, overwhelmed.

Her cheeks were flushed. "Hey, here's the thing," she murmured. "I'm on my period, so I can't do everything."

"Okay," he said, dazed.

"But we can still have some fun."

"Okay."

She chuckled and kissed him again so he felt the chuckle in his own throat. Her hand was on his chest, and he could feel his heart thump-thumping against it. He edged his hand to her waistband, felt the skin of her stomach moving, and she shook her head *no* against his mouth. "I'm too ticklish," she breathed. Instead he reached around her back and pulled her close. The slick Packers jersey was distracting, its mesh fabric, the vinyl iron-on of Bart Starr's name. But it was getting easier not to think about things. It was getting easier not to think about anything outside his body and hers and the places they touched each other: his lips, her lips; her hands, his chest; his dick, the leg she'd thrown over him. He knew by now she had to be aware of his boner, pushing hard into his boxers and jeans. What he wanted now was for something to push back against it, and as if reading his mind, she eased him back and climbed on top of him. Her mouth never left his. She was pulling something out of him with her breath and her hands and, yes, this was what he wanted, that pressure as she moved herself up and down.

From another room somewhere he heard a scuff, a thump. Laurie winced and exhaled and Kevin caught his breath, came back to himself. She tilted back on the fulcrum of her pelvic bone, lines appearing in her face as she looked at the door. Had the door been there before? He only remembered a jungle of ferns. "Is that your sister?" he asked.

She looked back at him, placed a finger on his lips. "I promise you she's not coming out," she whispered. "She's not dressed."

He grinned. "Sounds like *she*—" But the sudden blankness of her expression, as if desire had been wiped from her face with a cloth, stopped him short. Clearly he'd stepped wrong. He was about to say *Just kidding, just kidding*, but she rearranged her mouth back into the winning smile and brought her face down to his.

The instant their lips touched he lost himself again. She rocked slowly along his dick. They'd reached the part where their movements were not coincidental, where they were coordinating without speaking. She was pushing where she wanted to push, where he wanted her to push. She was moving with purpose, drawing everything—him, the candlelight, the room itself—into her with concentration. It was so different than it was with Theresa, who always let him take the lead, who—no need to think of her. They'd found a rhythm. She moved one of his hands around to her front, placed it square on the jersey's number 1. He could feel the softness of her breast underneath. He could feel one of her fingernails sharp at the base of his skull. She made a noise of encouragement in her throat that pulled him forward, into her somehow. Their boundaries were dissolving.

Then she grunted and turned her mouth away from his. Her face, in the candlelight, was alive with feeling, like a hundred faces at once. One of them was the person she'd been in the tavern. One of them was the person she was here. One of them was Theresa's, and one of them was dark and smeared.

He felt his breath return. He hadn't come—had been moving in that direction but hadn't quite gotten there. It seemed like Laurie had. She was breathing hard and resting her weight forward, catching his bladder, so he guided her away. Her face was familiar again, had settled back into itself after its moment of transfiguration. Kevin had never gotten a woman off that way. More accurate, he thought, would be to say that a woman had never gotten herself off on him that way. He had been helpful, it seemed: the hard place. Now that it was done, he couldn't tell if she even wanted him there. He wasn't sure if he wanted to be there. What had he seen, exactly?

She smiled. "Don't worry," she said. "I'll take care of you." She reached for her beer and took a sip. Another song started on the stereo.

There was a sound once again from deeper in the house, and she grimaced, then shrugged. "It's distracting having her back there, but it's her house, too."

"You're ready to get out."

"God. Yes." She already seemed far away. "I've got six months, maybe a year, helping my sister out, and then she'll be complete."

He might have wondered what she meant by *complete* but had really just been waiting until she finished because he'd thought of something he wanted to say. "It's like, you just have to put in the time sometimes. That's how it was for me and Theresa, I think. It was good that we were together so long. I learned something. I grew."

"Did she grow?" Laurie asked. The sister made a noise again, way off in the distance.

"What?"

"Theresa, or whatever. Was it good for her that you were together so long?"

"I mean, yeah. She's a nurse now," he said.

She nodded. She didn't seem satisfied with the answer, and he wondered if there was something she'd said that he'd missed. Theresa was always claiming he didn't listen, and it was true that sometimes toward the end of some declaration she'd been making he would realize he'd gotten lost and would have to scramble to respond. Like now, he realized, Laurie was just finishing a sentence: ". . . gets me closer to leaving."

"What gets you closer to leaving?"

She touched the front of his jeans. "Every guy who comes over."

He laughed uncertainly. He thought if he were more sober he definitely could figure out what she meant by that. She unzipped his fly and reached in but then gasped and drew her hand back as if burned. "You're wearing something she gave you?" she asked.

"Yes," he managed to croak. He could hardly breathe. The pressure in his chest, in his bladder, was unbearable. He stood up. "I gotta piss. Where's the bathroom?"

She sat up and brushed back her hair. "Down the hall on the left," she said. "Don't get lost."

He took a step toward the door and felt an uncomfortable tug on his boxers, like his dick was caught on something. He gave a little jostle. The candles on either side of the door had burned swimming pools of melted wax into their surfaces. As he opened the door he looked back and saw some indescribable expression moving over her face like weather. Had he fucked it up? If only he hadn't drunk that last beer.

Well, maybe he could salvage things. He was in a long hallway lined with framed photographs. The figures seemed to move in the candlelight.

This chick really loves candles, he thought. *That's cool.*

The bathroom on the left also held a flickering candle, but to his relief he also saw normal switches on the wall. He clicked one and the roaring shower fan kicked on. He cursed and turned it off. The other switch lit up the bathroom. He winced at the glare, winced again at the sight of himself in the mirror: flushed, lips red with lipstick, wet spot on the front of his pants. He remembered her promise to take care of him. He wondered what she'd do.

The bathroom was tidy and small, with a Stephen King book on the toilet's tank. Makeup and washcloths neatly arranged on the counter next to a clean sink; two toothbrushes in a metal holder; a little cactus in a pot on a footstool. The candle smelled like apple cider and bones.

Jesus, did he have to piss. He pulled his half-hard dick from the boxers and a blizzard of flannel fuzz wafted onto the toilet seat and floor. These goddamn underpants! He should've washed them before he wore them. Or he shouldn't have worn them at all.

On closer inspection, he discovered that the head of his dick was completely covered in black and blue fluff. "Huh," he said, his voice hollow against the tiles. He guessed the fuzz had gotten caked to his dickhole, stuck there by that wetness, the stuff that leaked out while they humped—the stuff *Forum* called "pre-cum." Bodies, man. Weird shit! He plucked at the cemented fuzz but now he could feel the urine coming, unstoppable thanks to his stance and the very presence of the open toilet before him, damn the torpedoes, he would just blast that funny flannel cap off the head of his dick with the power of four beers. Here it came.

Piss sprayed everywhere. Everywhere! *Everywhere!* All over the toilet tank! All over the book! Backward into his shirt! Straight up *into the air*, like a *sprinkler*, pattering the wallpaper with a sound like spring rain. He tried to clench to stop the flow, but he was helpless now—it was just coming and coming, splashing onto his *face*, and he grabbed at the head of his still-spraying dick, trying to pluck off the flannel plug. It didn't work, he just sprayed hot piss all over his hand, the mirror, the toilet paper. He crouched lower and lower, trying to catch it all inside the toilet bowl, but a new jet shot directly left as if from a poorly attached garden hose, arcing over the sink, extinguishing the candle with a hiss. He heard himself cursing, cursing, stumbling, knocking over the footstool and its cactus, which scattered gravel all over the now-wet floor.

From far away, he heard a voice. He couldn't distinguish it, but it wasn't hard to figure out what it was asking. It was asking if he was okay in there. "Everything's cool!" he shouted in what sounded to him like a very uncool voice. Finally, *finally*, he scraped the fuzz off, and his stream straightened just as it petered out. He looked down at his traitor penis, at the underwear that had ruined everything. In the toilet bowl, the fuzzwad floated, its damage done. Theresa had done this, he thought. Laurie had known. Theresa had reached out and touched him from far away with her gift, ensuring that though he might try to move beyond her, she would stay stuck to him, attached at his tender-est places.

He looked around at what he had done to the bathroom.

It was like a murder scene, but with pee. He could see spots on the *ceiling*. The cover of the book was soaked. Worse than that: the sink, her makeup, all the bathroom stuff, all dappled with piss. He blotted everything with toilet paper. He found Scrubbing Bubbles under the sink and cleaned everything as best he could. He wiped the counter, the mirror, poor *Cujo*. He rinsed out her makeup brush. He flushed, flushed again, the last of the TP headed down the pipe. He cleaned up the gravel, shoveled it back into the cactus pot, stabbed himself in the hand. At least her plant got watered, he thought, and coughed a bitter little laugh.

Last of all, worst of all, oh fuck: the toothbrushes. He stared at them, one blue, one yellow, standing at attention by the sink, covered in god only knew how much piss. He looked at himself in the mirror: his mess of a shirt, his overheated face. He knew that face; he knew what kind of person that was. He narrowed his eyes at himself. He'd never much liked his face, felt his eyes were too beady, too stupid look-ing, but he'd always thought it was the face of an honorable man.

This was a crucible. This moment would define him. He hadn't solved Laurie's problems. He hadn't solved Theresa's problems. He caused the problems—he *was* the problem. Could he walk away from this house knowing that these women would pick up these tooth-brushes and open their mouths and—it was too gruesome even to imagine.

But what was the alternative? To tell Laurie what had happened? To stand in that living room, illuminated by candles, listening to Don Henley, and tell her he'd pissed all over her bathroom and her tooth-brushes were now off limits?

Instead, he plucked the despoiled toothbrushes from their holder and buried them in the trash can under the Kleenexes and tampon wrappers, buried them so deep that, he hoped, they'd never be found—would simply be a mystery the women would never solve. It was better for them to wonder than it was for them to know something happened at all.

He picked up the soap and rinsed it off before he washed his hands with it. Then he washed them again. It was while he was washing for the third time that he finally, for the first time in what seemed like forever, glanced at his watch. It was nine fifteen, which meant he was more than half an hour late to meet the fucking kids at the fucking van.

It was as if a mist lifted. He caught his breath once and for all. What the hell was he doing in this bathroom? What was up with this weird woman who'd been dry humping him?

And what was that horrible groaning sound?

He burst out of the bathroom into the narrow hallway. There was a door at the far end of the hall now, open into a bedroom that looked more like a cavern, flame-lit and dripping, and standing in the cavern was a woman. The groaning was coming from her. She had a shape he couldn't understand, a color mottled and red, like raw hamburger left too long in the fridge. She was facing away from him but was beginning, with terrible purpose, to turn in his direction. With each move her skin—the skin—jiggled and sagged from her shoulders. Printed across her back he could see the letters G R E G G.

He shouted, maybe words. Pictures clattered off the wall as he fumbled behind him for the doorknob. Laurie's sister took a step toward him, took another. The skin she wore swayed in every direction like a loose skirt. She opened her mouth wide, too wide, and Kevin thought her groan might turn into roar, but instead she inhaled—her eyes bulging wide. Kevin felt his chest collapse as if someone were sitting

on him, felt the air rush from his lungs—and then he got the door open
and fell through it and slammed it behind him.

Laurie was still sitting on the couch. She looked miserable. "I
guess you're outta here, huh?"

Kevin gasped for air. "*Fuck!*" he managed to wheeze. A plant
brushed his cheek and he swiped at it. The vines tangled in his hand
and the pot smashed to the floor. Laurie winced.

"You never *listen*," she said in a rush. "You never *notice*." Her face
shifted one last time, into an expression of determination. "I have got
to get out of this house," she said, reaching for Kevin with her razor-
sharp nails. He leapt away, grabbed his coat, and ran. Ran through the
kitchen with its fresh pot of simmering lapskaus, the meat bobbing to
the surface. Ran through the front door with its tree-shaped knocker
even now howling like the wind. Ran into the cold, still wrestling the
coat over his arm, shocked sober and awake by the chill. He ran up
54th Street, ran away from that house and that bathroom and the
hags, his shoes kicking up ice and snow. He skidded around the corner at Hampton House. In the parking lot there were spatters of blood
on the snow. The kids were nowhere to be seen. The van, the van, was
gone.

He bent over, hands on his knees, weeping and gasping for air. He
thought he might never catch a full breath again. He heard from inside
Hampton House the muffled thumping of drums, the dampened wail
of guitar. "Go to Helen Waite," he said in despair.

SIGMONE AND JOEL

They'd barely made it two blocks when some pervert found them. He pulled up in a Chevy and called through an open window. "What are you boys looking for?" Thick glasses, sandy hair. Sigmone could see him drumming his fingers on the steering wheel. The boys walked a little faster, but the car kept pace alongside them. Joel muttered, "Let's turn here," and they cut across a corner yard to 57th.

The Chevy made the turn, too. "You guys lost?" the creep asked. "Come on in and warm up."

"No thanks," Sigmone said. All these years of his mom worrying about white men in cars and here it finally was.

"You better get in," the guy said, "or I'll make you."

Make them? There was someone approaching on the sidewalk, a bum it looked like, and the creep parked to wait him out. Sigmone and Joel picked up the pace. Sigmone glanced over his shoulder; the guy watched them, his face perfectly blank. Should they turn back to Hampton, try to find Kevin? That would mean walking right past the Chevy. What Sigmone wanted was an adult, a black adult best of all, someone who would take his side if the guy in the car said something. This bum was black but he did not seem promising. He had none of the authority of Sigmone's dad or grandfather, was scraggly and worn down, wore bib snowpants and a John Deere cap. He didn't even meet Sigmone's eyes. Sigmone decided that as soon as they got past the drunk he was going to take off running, into a backyard or something. He ran track. He could outrun some white guy in glasses.

As the bum passed them, Sigmone heard him mutter, "I see the monster calls."

Joel yelped. Sigmone was pretty sure the kid had never been so close to two black people at once. Behind them, pounding, shouting: The bum had planted himself directly in front of the Chevy and was smacking its hood over and over. "The MONSTER CALLS!" he shouted. The creep, astonished, stared up at him through the dirty windshield. The guy was straight up denting his hood. "You seek someone to DEVOUR? You are NOT WELCOME HERE!"

The perv threw it in reverse and backed away. The man raised his arms in the air and roared, *roared*, and the wind kicked up around him and made the mist seem to swirl. The headlights caught him and made him look for a moment radiant, lit up like the filament in a light bulb. The Chevy pulled away down the street, and the man's voice echoed through the block, sang from the bare trees: "BEGONE!"

The car begoned. The man stood, trembling, in the frozen street. Sigmone wanted to go to him but was sincerely afraid of the guy's juju. What *was* that he had done? Without a glance back at the boys, he stepped onto the sidewalk and continued walking away.

"Thank you, mister," Joel finally called. The man did not acknowledge him. "I am *not* telling my dad about this," he added.

Why had Sigmone become a paperboy? When he was eleven, his mom had put him in the car and driven what seemed like forever before they parked in an enormous lot, a sea of cars. It was the first mall he remembered ever seeing. Beautiful lights lined the balconies inside. Christmas music played everywhere. In the center of the mall stood a tall steel monolith, water cascading down its sides.

His grandfather was waiting by that fountain. His mom had seemed nervous beforehand, talking more than usual in the car, but she seemed to relax when she saw him. Sigmone remembered she kissed his grandfather, her father, on the cheek. He stooped down and looked Sigmone in the eye. "How you doin', little man," he said. His mom took a photo of the two of them in front of the fountain; later she would be furious when she got it back from the Kodak place and it hadn't turned out.

Used to be he saw his grandfather all the time, had even stayed with him while his parents went away. He lived alone, a few blocks from Sigmone's house. His grandmother, his mom's mom, had died before Sigmone was born. No one talked about her much. Sigmone saw how the people in the neighborhood acted around his grandfather, a little nervous, a little respectful, and how gruff the man was with them. He wasn't gruff with Sigmone, though he did talk to him like an adult.

His grandfather had owned a place on Capitol Drive, a storefront that sold cigarettes, hardware, kente cloth—a mix that Sigmone only now was starting to understand was unusual. When Sigmone was in fourth, fifth grade, he'd get off the 15 bus at the end of the school day and hang out in the store. There he'd sit around, open boxes of merchandise, sort nails into their little compartments. Kind of like he was helping Luis, his grandfather's only employee, but mostly he was getting in the way. Sometimes his grandfather asked him questions, but mostly the man just talked—talked about how things used to be in the neighborhood, and in Bronzeville, where Milwaukee's black folks had lived before. Talked about how the hoods were ruining everything now, still complaining even when those same young men came in to buy cigarettes.

But then his grandfather disappeared, for a time that seemed like forever but Sigmone now supposed was about a year. At the mall that day, he understood his grandfather was trying to show him a good time, to make up for how long he'd been away. He bought Sigmone a bag of roasted peanuts at Buddy Squirrel and—a miracle—a Paul Pressey jersey at Fan Fair. "Merry Christmas," his grandpa said, chuckling, as an excited Sigmone pulled it over his T-shirt and admired himself in the mirror.

The mall was decked out for the holidays, garlands and trees everywhere. Here and there gigantic foil-wrapped presents were piled in stacks, taller than his grandfather, as if the people walking the corridors were themselves gifts tucked under a tree. Screaming little kids lined up with their parents to see Santa Claus.

"You don't need to see him, right?" his grandpa said, and Sigmone knew the right answer was "No way," even though it did make him feel sad about not being little enough to do that anymore. When he'd been truly young enough to believe, his grandpa had been around all the time. They'd visit the Santa in Harambee every December. One year his grandpa had even been the Santa—had winked to Sigmone as he approached. Maybe his reappearance today meant that could happen again next Christmas.

They considered a movie, but nothing was playing that they really wanted to see. Sigmone remembered his grandfather joking about one of the titles on the marquee: "*Out* of Africa? I already know *that* story." Anyway, there wasn't time—they had to meet his mom soon. They walked to a back hallway where, to Sigmone's amazement, there was an arcade full of brand-new games, way better ones than they had in his neighborhood. They waited in line for Pole Position and his grandpa sat next to him in the dual drivers' seats. As they chose their cars, his grandpa pulled his sunglasses out of his breast pocket and slipped them on. It was corny but also cool. And then he smoked Sigmone in the race.

Looking for a game that no one else was lining up for, Sigmone found Paperboy. But Sigmone loved Paperboy. He'd played it on his friend Roman's Atari on one of his infrequent visits to Roman's house. There, he hardly got any time to play before his friend's anxious Russian mom ushered them outside. But here—his grandpa, amused, watched him steer the bike with the game's handlebars. "So really, all you're doing is throwing those newspapers?" He couldn't believe that was the game, but he slapped Sigmone's back when he broke the windows in the creepy old houses and laughed when Sigmone smacked into a car. When the game was over, the final screen displayed a newspaper's front page. AMAZING PAPERBOY DELIVERS! shouted the headline, with a picture of a freckled kid in a baseball hat. "Can I have another quarter?" Sigmone asked. His grandfather gave him two and went off to make a phone call.

Sigmone knew the game seemed silly to other kids. You weren't boxing Piston Hurricane or shooting aliens with a gun. But something about the geometry of it was so satisfying. He got the same feeling cruising on that bike that he got cruising down the track during a meet—the feeling he was untouchable. He loved swerving around the skateboarders and old ladies, loved darting a rolled-up newspaper straight into a postbox.

His grandpa returned in time to see Sigmone type his initials into the number six space on the score list. "All right, man," he said, and took Sigmone to the change machine, where he handed him a five-dollar bill. The landslide of quarters from the machine's mouth was extravagant, obscene. He couldn't believe he was allowed to take them all. He wished, now, that he'd been listening better to whatever it was his grandfather had said before he walked away, but he was so focused on the quarters weighing down the pockets of his jeans. Usually at the arcade, if you were crushing a game, you'd eventually draw a crowd, but not if the game was Paperboy. So no one saw him hit number five on the score list, then number three. He was right in the middle of his best run ever when his mom came running in crying and shouting and pulling him away from the game. She held him tight and, over her shoulder, he saw his paperboy slowly, slowly coast directly into the path of a car. He didn't even get to type in his initials.

Maybe that was why he'd gotten the delivery job, Sigmone thought, as he and the obnoxious Joel walked up 57th toward the addresses on their clipboard. Some kind of under-the-surface shit about that game, and how he'd never seen his grandpa again after that day. Or maybe he just needed money to keep up with the kids at the school he took the bus to every morning, and it wasn't like his mom and dad had a lot to spare. Whatever the reason, his experience was nothing like the towheaded kid in the video game. He didn't ride a bike down a sunny street. He didn't even have a bike. He delivered in the dark of morning, in the freezing cold, and mostly dropped the papers in the doors of local businesses: the hairdresser's, the Chinese restaurant, his grandfather's old store, now run by Luis, who'd managed to avoid getting tarred with the same brush. It was funny that the paperboy's neighborhood, with its beautiful houses, was such a danger zone. He wondered how that kid would do if you dropped him in Sigmone's part of town, where the traps and snares were less visible.

Joel was fretting about his boom box. Did Sigmone know this neighborhood? Was it safe to leave his boom box in the van? "I've never been in this neighborhood, either," Sigmone finally said. "But no one's gonna guess there's an expensive radio in that piece-of-shit van."

"Yeah, that's a good point, man," Joel said. Sigmone was already annoyed by him. He was a pain. But on the other hand, that boom box was deluxe, the nicest Sigmone had ever seen. He would love to crack it open and see how the CD player worked, watch the laser do its magic. Most of the kids at his school seemed sort of rich, but this kid was *actually* rich, mansion rich, and it wouldn't hurt for Sigmone to be nice to him for a while and see what happened.

The first house was around the corner. Joel said, "Here, listen to this," and then started beatboxing. Beatboxing! Sigmone looked around to make sure there was no one besides him witnessing this. "What are you doing?" he asked, but then the kid busted out rapping.

> *I walk through the jungle with my dick in my hand*
> *I'm the mean motherfucker from another land!*
> *I see a hundred naked ladies up against a wall*
> *I bet you fifty dollars I can fuck 'em all!*

Sigmone had stopped walking. Joel had a voice on him. It rang through the street. The last thing Sigmone needed was some neighbor hearing this crap and calling it in. Joel, too, had stopped walking, and was now grinning like the cat who got the canary, as Sigmone's mom liked to say. Here came the punch line.

> *I fucked ninety-eight, 'til my balls turned blue*
> *Then I took a shot of whiskey, and I fucked the other two!*

"Cut that shit out," Sigmone said.

"You don't think that's funny?" In a way Sigmone admired Joel's courage, to try that with a black guy he just met. Or maybe it was plain stupidity.

"Is that some Beastie Boys or whatever?"

"No, I made it up."

"You made that up."

"Some of it," Joel clarified. "The part about being a mean motherfucker. *A mean motherfucker from a distant land—*"

"Why's it gotta be the jungle?"

"It's like, Vietnam or whatever. You want to hear the rest?"

"There's more?"

Joel beatboxed again, as if letting the spirit recapture him. He seemed entirely unselfconscious, having the time of his life doing this on a frigid street in the middle of the night. He wore, Sigmone saw, a Swatch. He rapped, "I went to the doctor and the doctor said"—he dropped his voice way down low—"'I'm sorry, son, but your balls are dead.'"

Sigmone laughed. He couldn't help it.

He knew Joel. At least knew of him. They went to the same school, though Joel was in eighth grade and Sigmone was in seventh. Joel's mansion was in Whitefish Bay, right on the lake, and he probably got a ride to school in his dad's Porsche or whatever. Sigmone, meanwhile, rushed through his paper route so he could catch the 15 bus, which took him up through Shorewood and right by the school. His dad never got tired of telling him what a golden opportunity he'd been given, and he supposed he was lucky, though it didn't feel lucky to be one of three black kids in the entire class.

There were a lot of Joels at his school all of a sudden: white kids who'd just discovered rap. The variety show last spring had been a parade of Beasties, three different groups of boys in sideways Brewers hats lip-synching "Brass Monkey" or whatever. He could tell the teachers hated it and for once he agreed with them. The boys had started talking black with one another, and sometimes even tried it with Sigmone—for example when one of the groups, not the one Joel was in, asked him to join their act. It reminded him of how the kids who barely even looked at him in class got real interested once it was time to pick teams at recess.

He'd suggested to the variety show group that they should do LL Cool J instead. They said they didn't know any of his songs. He spent a lot of his time in Whitefish Bay just shutting the hell up.

The porch light was on at the first house on their list. Joel propped the storm door open with his elbow and pushed the doorbell. A single eye peered out from behind the frilly curtains. Sigmone backed up behind Joel, holding the clipboard in front of his body. An old white lady with wispy hair opened the door, holding on to her housecoat, flowery and loose like his aunt liked to wear. She looked right at Joel and did her best not to notice Sigmone. Joel started a sales spiel which, to Sigmone's relief, didn't include anything weird at all.

While he talked, Sigmone noticed the porch light, which didn't match the house. It was oversized and black, tricked out like it belonged on some fancy country club, not a little house way out here. But it was clearly cheap and plastic, and the bulb didn't sit right in the fixture.

The woman politely declined Joel's offer and started closing the door, but Sigmone stepped forward. "Hey, you need to get that porch light fixed," he said.

"Excuse me?" the woman said. Joel gave him a look like, *What are you doing?* Sigmone wondered himself, but he couldn't stand how bad that light was installed.

"You see how the bulb's crooked?" He leaned his head right against the house and eyed the fixture from the side. The bulb shone bright, 200 watts, he thought. It nearly touched the front of the plastic cube encasing it. "The socket's not installed right."

"My son just put it in," she said. "It's new."

"Yo, I'm sure her son knows what he's doing," Joel said. "Come on."

Sigmone ignored the *yo* and pointed to the light. "The bulb's heating that fixture up. Might cause a fire."

"A fire?" Now he had her attention. The woman opened the storm door and squinted. "It does look a little off," she admitted.

"You call your electrician," Sigmone said. "I bet your son just made a tiny little mistake. It was nice of him to put that in for you."

"I will," she said. "Thank you, young man."

"Yo, she should have bought a subscription, you basically saved her life," Joel said as they returned to the sidewalk. "How did you know all that?"

"My dad takes me on jobs sometimes," Sigmone said. "I'm good with electrical stuff." In fact, his teacher had basically made him the person in charge of the AV cart whenever she wanted to show a film-strip or video. It was him who made sure everything was connected; it was him who got to press the button advancing to the next slide, the job he'd always wanted in third grade but which made him faintly em-barrassed now. It did keep him from zoning out, though. His reward, she'd told him, was that at the end of the year he could pick out a movie for the class to watch, though she'd given him a whole lecture about how it had to be "something everyone will enjoy."

For his birthday his dad had given him a multimeter, which he'd used on every outlet in the house, and a book—the biography of Kareem Abdul-Jabbar, the Laker. Kareem had written it himself. "I thought you might want to see how another giant lives his life," his dad said. Kareem reclined on the paperback's cover, so tall his legs stretched around the spine and onto the back of the book.

Between his eleventh and twelfth birthdays Sigmone had grown almost a foot. People had always tried to get him to play basketball, but now everyone—classmates, teachers, the coach—*begged* him. He didn't like it that much, though of course he played. He did like Kareem—liked how reserved he was, as if he was just doing a job out there on the court. Sometimes, when no one was around, Sigmone tried a skyhook. He almost always bricked it.

He wasn't much for books and was a slow reader, but every night in bed he read a page or two. He skipped the parts about jazz, which he didn't care about, and drugs, which scared him. He reread the parts about the girls Kareem made it with about ten times. And for the first time in his life, he grabbed a pen and underlined something in a book:

what Kareem said about being tall and black. He'd felt a little thrill of disobedience making a mark in the book, even though he knew he was allowed—it was *his*. The line was something like, Kareem was big, but he never wanted to stand out, so he became an *observer*.

That was Sigmone to a T. If he went around acting all boisterous like Joel, other kids—hell, his teachers—would be scared of him. So in the past year or so he'd learned to watch. He watched the kids in his school. He watched his dad when he took him out in his truck, watched how he interacted with the neighborhood. He watched his own hands as he took apart and put back together the toaster, the coffeepot, the TV. And although he didn't understand everything, he learned from what he saw.

Now he watched Joel as the white kid chattered his way down the street, a running commentary of rap lyrics, insults about Kevin, and dirty jokes. His monologue only ceased when they reached a house and they both waited to see who would answer. If the person was white, Joel took the lead. If the person was black, Sigmone did. They didn't discuss this plan, just fell into it from the start. They didn't sell any subscriptions to anybody.

The neighborhood reminded Sigmone of his own—the houses were smaller, but there was a similar feeling of the people who lived here just barely keeping the world at bay. A few of the houses had junk all over the lawn, old mowers and table saws and shit, and then the house next door would sport a tidy flower box, as if it were telling the junk house off.

Once they struck out at a house, Joel went right back to talking. "If you like electronics, you should see the recording studio in our basement," he said. "Sometimes I help set up microphones and stuff."

"Why do you have a recording studio in your house?"

Joel looked embarrassed. "My dad's a musician."

"I didn't know they have rock stars in Milwaukee."

They turned the corner. "He's not a rock star," Joel began, but then Sigmone threw out an arm and stopped him.

Just a few houses away, standing in the middle of the street, was the biggest dog Sigmone had ever seen. Bigger than that mean German shepherd that his neighbor let roam his yard, who barked at Sigmone every morning and left dog-shaped dents in the fence. The huge dog in the street trotted to the sidewalk, moved from a streetlight to a dark patch, and stopped. It turned in their direction.

"Don't move," Joel muttered.

Sigmone *couldn't* move. The dog was staring right at him. All he could see from here was the glinting reflection in its eyes, but somehow he could feel those eyes lighting up his insides. The dog was a dark shape against dark shapes, but one that moved with intelligence and purpose. It was familiar to Sigmone, like a creature from his dreams. He heard Joel make a whimpering sound and felt the hairs on his arms and legs crackle.

Headlights silhouetted the dog's form. It whipped its head toward the car and then loped into a backyard. "*Jesus*, shit," Joel said, exhaling. "Was that a *wolf*?"

"He saw us," Sigmone said. The car rolled past them, and the street was once again quiet.

"That was like something out of a horror movie," Joel said. "Like, did you see *Teen Wolf*?"

"Do we have to go to that house? Where the dog went?"

"It's on the list," Joel said, perusing the clipboard. The house looked abandoned. An Oldsmobile, stripped for parts, sat up on blocks in the driveway, half covered by a tarp. "But I think we can skip it."

Next door their knock was answered by a white guy with a mustache and a Miller Lite T-shirt. He only sort of listened to Joel's spiel, but also seemed to be looking past them, up and down the block. Maybe he was searching for his giant-ass dog. "I already get the newspaper," he finally said. "Comes every afternoon."

"That's the *Journal*," Joel said. "We're selling the *Sentinel*."

"The morning paper," said Sigmone.

The man was already closing the door. "I don't need two papers."

"Hey wait," Sigmone said. "Does anyone live next door?"

"No," the man said flatly. "You don't want to go there." He turned off his porch light, leaving the boys in darkness.

"Okay! Good decision, I guess," said Joel.

On the way to the next house, Joel started recounting the plot of *Teen Wolf*, which sounded like some bullshit to Sigmone. "You really believe in that supernatural stuff?" he asked finally.

"Science cannot explain all that happens in the dark of night," said Joel. Sigmone sang the *Twilight Zone* song.

At the next house, their unspoken delegation of tasks faltered when the door was opened by an interracial couple. "Uh, hey there," Joel said.

Sigmone stepped forward, smooth as when he grabbed the baton in the 4x400. "We're selling subscriptions to the *Milwaukee Sentinel*," he said, and the couple smiled and opened up. The white lady held on to her husband's arm, and when Sigmone was done, they nodded to each other.

"Seems like a good idea," he said. Sigmone took their cash and handed it to Joel, who slid it into the envelope. The man even shook Sigmone's hand.

As they walked away, Joel said, "I'm just wondering, why'd you interrupt me there?"

"C'mon," Sigmone said. "It worked, didn't it?"

"No, I'm just asking a question here. Why can't anyone talk to anyone?"

"We're gonna have better luck if I talk to the black folks. You know that."

"I think you should let me talk to the next black, uh, black folks."

Just his luck to get the one white kid who thought he was down. To change the subject, he said, "So your dad isn't a rock star. Is he a country singer?"

Joel sighed. "No. You know what new age music is?" Sigmone gave him his most practiced blank look. "It's like, crystals and stuff. Acoustic guitar. Real mellow."

"Uh-huh."

"*I* think it sucks," Joel assured him. "My dad writes it. Anyway."

"People buy that crystal music? Enough people so you can live in that house?"

"There's a whole record label that does it. But that's not why we have the house. That comes from my grandpa."

"But you are rich."

"We're *comfortable*," Joel said with a practiced air.

"If you're so *comfortable*, why do you have a paper route?"

"My dad makes me do it. He says it's *important* to have a job growing up."

Sigmone shook his head. "That's just sad," he said. "I get rich, I'm gonna let my kids sleep in."

"My grandpa made him do it when he was a kid." He did the voice of a grandpa, sounding surprisingly like Sigmone's grandfather: "'Builds character.'"

"Getting up at five in the morning to build character? There's nothing important about getting up at five in the morning."

"Tell me about it." They walked a few steps in blessed silence, until Joel finally said, "What about *your* dad? Is it true about him?"

Sigmone stiffened up. "Is what true?"

"That he was, like, a witness in court."

"So you do know me."

"I've seen you in school. People say he was, like, against the gangs."

Sigmone stopped in front of the next house on the list. "People should shut up," he said.

"It's fine, forget it," Joel said. "I'm sorry." He walked up the path alone and rang the doorbell to the new-looking house, bigger than the ones surrounding it. A black man opened the door and looked at Joel standing there on the porch, Sigmone standing way back on the sidewalk. Joel barely said three words before the man shut the door in his face. As he walked back down the walkway Joel's look was so hangdog Sigmone almost felt bad about laughing.

"I guess I deserved that," Joel said.

"You sure did."

And now the floodgates were open. Joel felt comfortable asking him any old question in between people turning them down for subscriptions. "Do you have to choose between the Crips and the Bloods?"

"Those are LA gangs, come on."

"But there's Milwaukee gangs?"

"There's some guys on my block, but they leave me alone."

"Why?"

"Because I go to the white school."

"What music do you listen to? Do you hate the Beastie Boys because they're white?"

"They're all right," Sigmone allowed. The way Joel beamed! "LL's better. And Public Enemy. But I also like New Edition, Bobby Brown. And I listen to gospel."

Joel threw his hands in the air and shouted, "Amen!"

There was something refreshing about Joel's complete lack of manners. He was so obsessed with blackness—and so rich and uninhibited, Sigmone guessed—that he actually *talked* about race, instead of clamming up whenever the subject arose, like everyone else. Even

Sigmone's teachers, every last one of them white, had nothing to say about black people, and if you pressed them they'd surely say that oh, they didn't see color. It was just that some of their students came from, ya know, different parts of the city.

"It wasn't my dad," Sigmone said. He wondered which of the eighth-grade black kids had blabbed about it, because no way Joel heard about it otherwise. But he did feel the need to set him straight. "It was my grandpa."

"Okay."

"He went in front of a judge and testified." Sigmone's mom or dad usually picked him up by five thirty, so he wasn't there when a couple of neighborhood guys held the place up one night. Luis survived the shooting—they visited him in the hospital—but he wouldn't tell the cops who did it. Sigmone's grandfather, though: He told. Then he took off. Sigmone's dad boarded up the front window with its bullet holes until Luis fixed it and opened back up.

"Well, that's good, right?" Joel asked. "They got the bad guy."

"Not everyone thought it was good." For a while Sigmone had harbored a fantasy that his grandpa was out kicking ass like an action hero, but that story had been too pathetic to maintain, even in secret. He had his mom, and he had his dad, and he was doing a damn sight better than plenty of kids, as his parents never stopped reminding him. "How about *your* dad?" he asked. If Joel could get a crash course in being black, then Sigmone could learn what it was like being rich. "Do you have servants, like the Drummonds?"

"My dad has people who work for him, but they don't, like, take care of me."

"Oh yeah? Who cooks?"

"Alex."

"And who's Alex?"

"The chef who works for my dad."

Sigmone laughed. "Do you have actual silver spoons?"

"Dude, I don't know what our spoons are made of. Ask a real question."

"Your mom doesn't even cook?"

Joel shook his head. "My mom died when I was born."

"Oh shit, man, I'm sorry." Joel waved him off. They failed to make another sale, and then Sigmone looked for safer territory. "What kind of car does your dad drive?"

Here, Joel had expertise. "We've got two. A BMW E30, it's blue with leather interior. And he's got a black Porsche 911 Carrera."

Sigmone stopped in the street as sharply as he had when he'd seen the wolf. He considered himself a car guy, in part because his dad let him drive the truck around the Pick 'n Save parking lot now and then. "You actually have a Porsche," he said.

"A convertible."

"Are you gonna get to drive it when you get your license?"

"No way," said Joel. "He'd rather die. It's like in *Ferris Bueller* when Cameron says his dad loves his car more than life itself."

"I never saw that movie."

Now it was Joel who stared, shocked. "Oh, man, don't you see anything?"

"There's no movie theater by my house."

"You gotta see it. Ferris skips school for a day, and he gets to be in a parade, he's on TV, he gets to drive the car. And he gets away with it!"

"Sounds like a great movie about being rich."

"It's realistic."

"Stuff in movies doesn't happen in real life," Sigmone said. "I tried that in real life, I'd get expelled."

A white lady turned them down, saying, "Should you boys be out this late?" Joel said, "Ma'am, we couldn't agree more. But they won't let us back into the van unless we sell enough subscriptions." The lady just closed her door.

"I guess you're right," Joel said as they stepped off the porch. "But things go wrong for me just the same as you."

"Do you get to eat at Burger King all the time?"

"No, like, that's what I'm talking about. Alex cooks these healthy meals with bean sprouts and things."

"That's sad. That's truly sad."

"I'm telling you what it's like. I bet you get to eat fast food all the time."

"We get McDonald's two or three times a week."

"See, you're lucky."

Sigmone had to agree with him there. Bean sprouts! What the hell.

Joel started telling a whole long-ass tale—it took, like, four houses—about he and a friend chucking water balloons at cop cars in Whitefish Bay. In Joel's telling, they'd led the police on a chase over fences and through backyards. "Eric got caught because he was running through some bushes, see, and there were thorns, and the thorns ripped his shorts and ripped open his nutsack"—Sigmone was laughing now but Joel just kept on going—"and one of his balls fell out and it bounced on the ground."

"You're crazy."

"That's where Superballs come from."

"You didn't get caught."

"I hid under a boat in Bill Orchard's yard."

The kid from the Paperboy game would be fine, in the end, even if you dropped him on Holton Street in the middle of the night. Sigmone knew it. His freckles would protect him.

They'd crossed off most of the houses on their list, because it didn't really take that long for a person to say no. It didn't seem like they were gonna win the twenty bucks. Sigmone guessed they'd just go back to the van and wait in the cold for everyone else to return, probably with dozens of sales. One of the last addresses was a white house with a neatly maintained yard. As soon as they set foot on the front walk, a light flipped on in the tree above, bathing them in white, illuminating the patchy snow and the little blue flowers poking up here and there, a winter bloom. They must have some kind of fancy motion detector. Joel knocked twice before they heard the latches and dead bolt turn. Someone was saying, "It's okay, it's just some kids," and then a pretty woman with natural hair greeted them.

"We're selling subscriptions to the *Milwaukee Sentinel*," Sigmone said. "It's only ten dollars for three months, and if you subscribe for a year, you get a special plate."

"A commemorative plate," Joel added.

The woman smiled at Sigmone. He was flustered by how pretty she was. "The *Sentinel*, huh," she said. "I can't say I need any new plate."

Sigmone hunted for the perfect line. "Well," he said, "you can still get the newspaper, you know, for the news." Joel looked at him like, *That's what you came up with?*

She leaned against the doorframe and crossed her arms. She seemed to be playing with him, just a little. "I get my news from more trusted sources than the *Milwaukee Sentinel*," she said. "They really got you out in this neighborhood selling newspapers in the middle of the night?"

Joel put on his saddest voice. "Yes ma'am," he said.

The woman stayed focused on Sigmone. "Do you get a bonus or something, the more you sell?"

"Our manager says whoever sells the most gets twenty bucks."

"Huh." She picked up a purse from a table by the front door and rummaged through it. She was small and sharp-edged, darker than Sigmone. She pulled out two ten-dollar bills and handed one to each boy. "I don't need to give money to the newspaper, but you all can just have these."

"Whoa, thanks," said Joel. Sigmone echoed the thanks, but distractedly. He felt a presence in the next room, another person approaching. The presence itched at him. There was a hole in him where this person should go. He tried to peer around the edge of the door to see.

A man's voice rang out. "Who that at the door?"

"Just some young salesmen," she sang, with a wink to the boys. "I'm sending them on their way."

"We shouldn't be opening the door to any old visitor," the voice said. And then the voice was a man in the doorway, and Sigmone had an answer for the question his body had been asking.

"Grandpa?"

The man had a new beard and a new scar down his cheek, but it was him. Sigmone felt like he must be in a fairy tale or something.

The woman looked from Sigmone to his grandfather and back. "This is him?"

"How are you here?" his grandpa asked. He looked stunned. No—he looked angry. "How are you here right now?"

She smiled grimly. "Don't want surprises, you better not move to Hampton Heights," she said. "You all better come in."

Inside, Joel hopped up and down with excitement as the two adults went farther into the house to talk. "This is *insane*," Joel whispered, or tried to whisper. It came out more like a screech. "Isn't this insane?" Sigmone wished he would shut up so he could think.

The front door was closed and bolted behind them. The front hall opened onto a living room in one direction and a dining room in the other, both decorated simply. A Pan-African blanket draped over an easy chair. A small table set for two. Somewhere behind the dining room, his grandfather and the woman were arguing. He didn't know why they'd bothered withdrawing; the house was so small that he and Joel could hear them just fine.

"You cannot just put him out into the night," she said. "Not tonight."

"What's tonight?" asked Joel. Sigmone waved him off.

In the other room, his grandpa said, "This is my problem to solve."

"My house, too. My front door." He heard a familiar sigh of exasperation, the same sound his grandpa used to make when Sigmone got bored and started messing around in the store. "Don't you give me that," she warned. "Augustin, he's here for a reason. What do you think that is?" Augustin was his grandpa's middle name. In the neighborhood he went by Charles.

"How am I supposed to know?"

"Well, you gotta figure it out."

"Let's go," Sigmone said to Joel, who was nearly vibrating. His grandfather didn't want him here and he didn't want to be here. He didn't need this. But then there were footsteps, and the two adults returned to the front hall. The woman put her hand on Sigmone's shoulder. "I'm Kamika. You boys come in and sit down."

"I'm Joel," blurted Joel.

"Take your shoes off first, okay?"

Sigmone had spent a lot of time preparing things to say when he finally saw his grandfather again. He'd played out whole conversations in his head, in which he explained exactly how he felt about him leaving them, about how it felt to live in Harambee with his grandpa's offense blinking over him like a neon sign. Now, sitting at the dining room table as his grandpa carried in two folding chairs, he found himself utterly without words. His grandpa wore a work shirt and jeans. The scar on his face stretched from his right ear to his cheek, where it disappeared into a salt-and-pepper beard.

"You got tall," his grandpa said, making eye contact with Sigmone for the first time since he came to the door. "My mama's people were tall, too." When the chairs were set up, he finally sat down.

Kamika was still standing. "You boys want some soda?"

Sigmone said, "No thank you" as Joel said, "What kind do you have?" She brought out two cans of Coke. Sigmone popped his and took a drink. He was waiting, he realized. He was waiting for his grandpa to say something real.

"How is it that you two ended up in this neighborhood?" he finally asked. That wasn't it, so Sigmone stayed silent.

Joel looked at them both and said, "Our manager just gave us a printout." He held up the clipboard. "This was one of the addresses on it."

Sigmone's grandpa shook his head. Then he looked at Sigmone, really looked, and seemed to register him for the first time. "I'm not mad at you," he said. "I'm glad to see you, Sigmone." Sigmone didn't move, did his best not to respond, but he felt that in the same place inside his body where he'd felt his grandfather's presence. "It's just that this isn't a great time to be knocking on doors. What kind of sense of this neighborhood you get, walking around?"

Joel said, "Poor," as Sigmone said, "Like half black, half white."

His grandpa nodded. "Kamika grew up here."

"We were the first black family on this block." She sat down, holding her own Coke. Sigmone noticed she hadn't brought one for his grandfather.

"Who was here before?" Sigmone said.

His grandfather waved his hand. "Before. Well, the animals were here before. The Indians were here. The Kickapoo, the Potawatomi." Sigmone started to nod, like *You know what I meant*, but his grandpa cut him off. "It was their land, still is their land. I ain't saying that you got wendigos or hodags still running around, but the paths they walked, those are our paths, too."

"Abso*lu*tely," Joel said.

Sigmone's grandpa barely glanced at him. "But then the neighbor-hood was German. Farmland, then a village. It was called Granville. Maybe twenty years ago black folks started coming, when Bronzeville got torn down for the expressway. There were good factory jobs up here."

"I wonder how the white folks felt about that," Sigmone said.

"It wasn't as bad as some places," Kamika said. "No one's hold-ing hands and singing, but most people just stick together and don't bother anyone else."

"But things are changing. They used to make drill bits right down the street. That closed. There's less to go around, and, you know—" He snapped his fingers. "Conflict flares up, like a match."

Kamika nodded. "Sometimes when things get bad, that's when your grandpa and his crew step in."

Sigmone sat up straight, all his foolish hero fantasies rushing back. "Your crew?" He could just tell Joel was about to say something stupid about Crips and Bloods and dealt him a quick look to tamp him down.

His grandpa got up from the table and looked out the window. The light in the front yard had turned itself off, and there was nothing to see, just the islands of illumination cast by the streetlights. He turned and gave a look to Kamika, who threw her hands up in the air. "What you want, a written invitation?" she said.

Sigmone knew this feeling, watching this man decide whether to bother talking to his grandson, who came from miles away and, somehow, found him here. It was powerlessness. He couldn't make his grandfather care about him. It was how he felt so much of the time. Knowing his dad was at work all hours, fixing things in the houses of people who knew what his own family had done. Knowing his mom wanted only one thing from him, for him to go to college and get away from them. Staring out the window of the bus to the suburbs, watching the houses get bigger and the lawns get greener. Sitting in class, staring at the page, the words squirming before his eyes.

This fall his teacher had made the class read *Romeo and Juliet* out loud. Hearing a story was much better than reading it, and his class was full of loudmouths who volunteered for every role. But this time Ms. Schulz assigned characters out of a hat, and Sigmone ended up playing some guy called Tybalt, who had a lot of lines, and his reading was so quiet and halting that it brought the play to a standstill every time it was his turn. No one said anything, but Sigmone could feel the pity and scorn in the air. When he heard Chris McSorley muttering to his friends, doing an impression of slow Sigmone reading like some kind of moron, he shoved Chris into the lockers as hard as he could. So then he had in-school suspension, even though the week before Jason Kriefall had straight-up punched a kid and only got detention.

"Of course they're gonna punish you worse," his dad said. "What kind of world do you think you're living in?" He had to ride the bus to school just to spend the whole day in the conference room by the vice principal's office. Outside the closed door he heard the business of the school day: bells ringing, students complaining, younger kids out on the playground. Inside he had nothing but a book he didn't want to read and homework he didn't know how to do.

They didn't even let him go to track practice. And then the next day he was even farther behind. The only good thing was that Ms. Schulz had to make someone else play Tybalt.

Even now he thought about the look of fear on Chris McSorley's face when he hit the lockers. Even now he thought he could feel that powerlessness inside him, assuaged not even a little bit by what he did. It was an awful presence inside him, a thing alive.

Now Sigmone's grandpa said, "What sports do you play?"

"Uh, basketball. And I run track."

"What's your best sport?"

"It's track," Joel said. "He's fast as—he's really fast."

Sigmone's grandpa looked at Joel for the first time and nodded. Joel might as well have had a light bulb inside his head, the way he glowed. God, this guy had it bad.

"That true?" his grandpa asked.

"Yeah, I guess," Sigmone said. It really was no contest. He'd gone to county as the anchor in the 400 relay. It took until the county meet to face a school that could build a lead big enough that Sigmone couldn't erase it on the last leg.

His grandfather stood in the doorway now, blocking the light from the front hall. He seemed bigger now, bigger than Sigmone, but that was a trick of perspective. "How do you feel when you run?" he asked.

"How do I . . ."

"How do you *feel*," his grandfather intoned, "when you're at your *fastest*?" Sigmone felt a tug deep within. It came from his grandfather's eyes, which gleamed in the light from the chandelier.

He took a breath. "I feel powerful. Like no one can even touch me. Like I know exactly where to go and how to get there."

His grandpa nodded, as if Sigmone had passed some test. He couldn't imagine what it could have been. But his grandpa said, "Come on out back with me. You can do something, and I'm going to show you how." Sigmone let himself yearn, just for that moment, to know his grandfather, and for his grandfather to know him.

And that's when Joel went nuts. "Oh *shit!*" he shouted, punching Sigmone on the arm. "He's gonna show you how to be a *werewolf!*"

"Shut *up*," Sigmone said, at the exact moment that his grandpa said "Goddamn it," and Kamika started laughing. His grandpa stalked out of the room. Kamika was nearly doubled over. She called to him but could not keep it together. "Augustin! Come on!"

"What are you—"

"I could tell he wanted to do a big unveiling or whatever, in the backyard," Kamika said, going after him.

"I knew it!" Joel was up out of his chair and bouncing around the dining room. "That giant beast thing! And he's all mysterious! He's got a *crew*, like, that's his pack!"

Kamika pulled Sigmone's grandpa back into the room. He was clearly annoyed, which just made her laugh harder. "The *term*," he said, trying to recollect his former dignity, "is *wearg*."

Sigmone said, "Man, go to hell," his chair clattering behind him. He could barely see where he was going through the tears but he didn't care, he just wanted to be out of this stupid house, away from his stupid grandpa. He wanted to get the hell away from Hampton Heights, the place that had returned his grandfather into his life, unwilling, unsmiling, talking like a fool.

The problem was his shoes were off. He plucked them off the hall floor and just walked out the door. The front step was freezing through his socks. Halfway down the walk he stopped and tried to balance on one foot to pull on a shoe. His grandpa had followed him and was saying his name, something he'd wanted to hear forever, "Sigmone" in his grandpa's deep voice, but now he lashed out with all the courage he could muster. "You've been gone for*ever*!" he shouted. He gave up on the shoe and let it fall to the ground. His voice cut through the silent chill of the night. "I've been waiting! And I find you by accident and you don't even want to see me and you make up this stupid story." His grandpa was smiling now, hands on his hips. "You think this is funny?" Sigmone felt huge in his rage. "I wanted my grandpa! Not a bunch of bullshit! I wanted YOU!"

As he shouted the last few words, his grandpa's eyes glinted. Then Sigmone was on all fours, howling his sorrow and anger at the sky.

And he knew, *knew* instantly, that this was what he had felt when he'd seen his grandfather in the middle of the road, what he had felt when he sensed his grandfather in the house. It was the unseen thing, the ancient thing, tugging at his heart.

His feet were no longer cold. But there were more of them. He felt perfectly balanced, ready to spring. And there was his grandpa, his scent sharp and familiar. His face was triangular, his teeth long. It felt good to launch himself at him, to clamp his fur in his teeth, to snarl. But his grandfather turned him over. The world upside down, Sigmone on his back. His grandfather snapped at him. Instantly Sigmone cowered and apologized, his anger gone as if blown away in the wind.

The world was paler and smaller through his eyes. But it didn't even matter because now his nose and ears brought him such riches. Faraway danger, the roots creeping underground, the snow coming soon. Water in the distance. Paths and barriers in every direction, clear and easy to read. The boy, Joel, bursting out of the house and stopping and shouting. Even from here Sigmone could smell the thrill on him.

The big one took off running and Sigmone followed. They left the house behind because it was no longer theirs. The grass crunched underfoot. He cleared fences at a bound. His path was marked by the scents laid out by his grandpa and many others. The trails criss-crossed one another, and here and there Sigmone sensed places he wasn't meant to go, routes he wouldn't follow. And underneath, the tracks burned into the earth by centuries of people, the deep memory of the land.

For just a few steps, *pat-a-pat-a-pat*, the ground was hard under his feet: a road. Then he followed his grandfather at a trot down a long embankment to a stream. Here he could smell that people of every sort used this place to get water—he saw their trails everywhere and knew which people were small, which were big, which he needed to beware, which he could eat. The trails all converged on the brook as it burbled bright and cold through the snow and slush. His grandpa stopped to drink so Sigmone did, too, his fur brushing against his grandfather's as they stood side by side.

And then there was another, on the other side of his grandpa. The big one was not alarmed so he, too, wasn't alarmed, not even when a second person silently slipped next to him, or when a third sniffed him and nosed his side. He was new to the pack. He saw how they surrounded his grandfather, how alert each was to his surroundings. Each drank his fill in turn, paws sinking into the snow, tracks mixing with the paw- and hoof- and footprints dotting the riverbank.

Sigmone watched them all.

One lifted a leg at a tree. One bounded after a rabbit. They were gray and white and black. He could see that each person made his own choices but that all those choices were influenced by his grandfather—made to fit in the shape the big one established for all of them. His grandfather was the hill, and they were the trees arranged upon that hill. Each person was his own creature but was also ready at any moment to respond if his grandfather required it. And so when his grandpa lifted his head to sniff at the air and then trotted back up the embankment, each member of the pack turned away from whatever task had been occupying him and followed. Sigmone found his place at the corner of the group. And then they were running again, at the edge of the road, parallel to the stream, and Sigmone was filled with a sense of power.

The pack flowed like water across the snow and Sigmone was a part of it. They crossed the road, slithered single file between bushes. In a flat plain surrounded by hedges they gathered around Sigmone's grandpa. At the far corner of the space a pair of people stood at alert. The wind brought Sigmone fresh information: These people were like them but not like them, could change like them but were not part of their pack. They were not enemies, but they were not friends.

Sigmone's grandfather yipped once, then led the pack in a slow, wide circle. They hugged the line of hedges that held the plain within. The heads of the others followed them along their path. Now there were three there. Now there were four. They were also gray and white and black yet different in some indisputable way. The tracks and scents scattered across the ground here were wild and confusing: this was a border, a zone where the conflicts of this place got negotiated.

One of the others leapt forward, and Sigmone's grandpa sprang toward him, and then they were bounding alongside each other, snow and dirt flying. Sigmone might have thought they were playing but for the bared teeth. He didn't know what this fight might look like, had no sense of how far it could go, but he found he was not afraid. His confidence in the big one was absolute.

One person snapped, the other plowed into him; they were a whirl of fur and teeth. It happened too fast for Sigmone to catch it, but with a cry the other person ducked away. Sigmone could smell the blood from where he was standing, just a few drops spattering the snow.

Sigmone's grandfather stood in the center of the space, neck bristling. The other person retreated, favoring a foreleg, the other streaked red. He retreated through a hole in the hedge and was followed by the other pack. Sigmone's grandpa barked and chased, and soon they all stood in a new space behind a house. Sigmone could tell that this space was not theirs—was not theirs at all. But they spread to all corners and marked while they could: Sigmone pissed on something rusted and metal, another person on a small building, another on a circle of sand. From a ledge attached to the large house at one end of the space the injured one watched them decorate the yard. Finally he turned and limped into the house. The pack surrounded Sigmone's grandfather. He howled and they all joined him. What a noise! What a sound! It carried into the sky, seemed to bounce off the moon and return to them.

A car stopped for them as they crossed the road. The man in the car stared at the line of people in his car's lights. Sigmone looked the man straight in the eyes and he saw him flinch.

What the nature of this victory was, Sigmone did not know. His grandfather didn't suddenly own the house. Sigmone may have made his mark, but that yard wasn't his, he could sense that. The confrontation, the brief fight, the sharp scent of the urine—all those things had meaning far beyond themselves, having to do with subtle dynamics he, a stranger to this place, did not understand. There were rules that everyone else knew, and those rules had changed ever so slightly as a result of what he'd seen, what he'd done. He understood this at least.

He also understood that whatever comprehension he had of all this—the tracks in the snow, the sounds his pack made, the boundaries and paths—would fade when he stood upright again.

For now, he didn't care. For now, he ran, and felt the joy and power of running.

The rabbit was bright as a shooting star, bolting across the grass just ahead of him. Its fear made it stand out against the blank nighttime. Sigmone veered away from his pack and loped after it, feeling his legs stretch. He didn't want to eat it, exactly. But he did want to chase it, to test himself against it, to feel its heart beating, its crunch. It zigzagged away, lightning against the grass. It was headed for the far corner, a wooden barrier, and he pushed to get there first.

He did not. The rabbit squirmed between two pieces of wood—an opening much too small. He yelped, he leapt. It happened before he even knew he was going to do it. As he soared over the wooden barrier he saw the rabbit down below, wriggling back through the hole in the other direction. By the time he landed and gathered himself it was gone.

Never mind! Look what he could do! Snow flew as he sprang forward. Ahead was another, taller fence. He jumped over that one, too, dancing a few steps along the top just because he could. He landed next to a house, and suddenly his senses were shouting at him, because there were three new people next to the house.

The people turned as one and looked at him. They were lined up next to a car with no wheels, lifeless and dark. He wasn't afraid. He stood his ground while they approached him. He let them sniff. He did not make himself small. And the people didn't growl or raise their hackles. They circled him a few times, then broke off and moved together toward the house. No one of them led the group. Sigmone wondered how they knew what to do. At ground level there was a broken opening to the house, bright light inside, and one by one they disappeared into it. On the way in, the last person looked back at him. An invitation.

Sigmone was not frightened. He was curious. So he walked to the opening, pushed himself through, and braced himself for the landing.

The people were humans now. He shied away from their scents, their upright forms. One of them stepped forward and said, "You can change here."

Could he? Did he even know how? How would he appear? But then before he even finished asking the questions, he was human again. In a moment of panic he looked down at himself, but there were his clothes, his coat, even the shoes he hadn't managed to get on in his grandpa's front yard.

"You're new," a girl said, lighting a cigarette.

"Finally," one of the boys said. "Some fresh meat around here."

They stood in a triangle in the empty basement, lit by a camping lantern on the floor. A white girl and two boys, one white, one black. They looked to be a couple years older than him. They were dressed like the high school burnouts who skulked past him at the bus stop by his school: dark jeans, trench coats over T-shirts. The white guy, who'd just spoken, had hair so curly and poofed up he looked like a poodle.

"Did we ever work out what happens to our clothes when we change?" the girl asked her friends now.

"Nope," said the black guy. He had a high fade and a flat top. Sigmone eyed his shoes; he didn't know if he'd ever seen a brother wearing combat boots like those. "I guess it's just"—here he raised an eyebrow dramatically—"*ancient magic*." The three of them laughed.

"Once I was wearing earrings when I turned, and when I turned back I only had one of them," said the other guy. "Totally different look."

"You all, what, a gang?" Sigmone asked.

"Yeah, one of those interracial gangs," the black guy said. "Like in Spider-Man."

The teens smiled at one another, some private language. "Just stealing purses in dark alleys," said the white kid. "I'm Justin." The girl, his sister, was Jenny. The black guy was Greg.

Sigmone introduced himself. The good thing about being tall was people didn't necessarily know right away you were barely thirteen.

"How'd you get here?" Greg asked. In a dark corner of the room Justin was messing with something, which turned out to be a radio. Finally, music came on, some kind of fast rock and roll.

Sigmone explained about the canvassing, about how against all odds he had stumbled upon his grandpa. They all laughed. "Fuckin' Hampton Heights," Justin said.

"It's like the crossroads," Greg agreed.

"One time I was just trying to get my hair cut and the ghost of my grandma kept blocking the razor," Jenny said. "I had to be like, 'Grandma, just let me get the buzz.'"

"Then she comes complaining to me," said Justin. "I'm like, 'Granny, she doesn't listen to me, either.'"

"What's funny is the ghosts don't care if we smoke," said Greg.

Jenny took a drag. "No, they love it. 'Join me in the afterlife!'" They all spoke airily, half-grinning, in such a way that Sigmone could not guess if what they were saying was real or a story they liked to tell one another. It was a kind of code, but unlike at school when kids told inside jokes, Sigmone didn't feel made fun of. Instead, he wanted to find a way in.

"So we roamed around the neighborhood, I guess," Sigmone said. "My grandpa got into a tussle, sort of, with another wolf."

"Did you know?" Greg asked. "Before tonight?"

Sigmone shook his head. "I didn't know anything."

"You never been in Hampton Heights before."

"Does it only happen here?"

"I never turn when I'm somewhere else," Jenny said. "It's real weird the first time. It's like it's all new but, also, like you've been doing it all your life but you didn't know it."

"And did you like it?" Greg asked.

Sigmone was thinking about the kinship he'd felt as part of that pack. He couldn't remember exactly how they'd communicated or what it had all meant, but that feeling had stuck with him. He had belonged. There was no fumbling for comprehension, no switching how he talked or acted based on who he was with. He had a kind of power among them, those wolves. Sometimes in his everyday he felt something like that, when he flipped a circuit breaker and saw the lights come to life, or when he made the turn and saw the finish line ahead and picked off his opponents, one by one. But he never felt it with anyone else, only alone, and most of the time he had nothing backing him up as he struggled to read in class, walked the streets of his neighborhood before dawn, rode the bus home as the afternoon faded away.

"I liked it," he said. "I wish I understood how it all happened."

"My friend, that question is irrelevant in our part of the world," said Justin. He offered Sigmone a cigarette, and Sigmone awkwardly declined. "Okay, don't give yourself cancer, see if I care," he said, but cheerfully.

"It's a little bit mind-blowing," Greg said.

"Yeah. Partly just the wolf thing"—they all laughed and Sigmone nodded, acknowledging that this was a funny thing to say—"but partly because my grandpa was, like, the *leader.*"

Justin and Jenny looked at each other, quickly, but not so quickly that Sigmone didn't notice. "Your grandpa's Augustin," Greg said.

"Yeah." Sigmone shook his head at the weirdness of it all. "That's what he goes by here, anyway."

Jenny pulled a raggedy lawn chair from the wall. The chair gave a tiny shriek of pain as she opened it. "*Our* dad is . . . the leader, I guess, of the vargr," she said, sitting down.

"The white wolves?"

"Yeah, although really all the wolves have the same color fur," Greg said.

"I noticed that," said Sigmone. "That shit's confusing."

"Tell me about it, man."

No one spoke for a moment. Greg pulled another chair out and sat down. He nodded at the cooler at Jenny's feet and she tossed him a soda. From the boom box, a man and a woman sang together, each one's voice winding around the other's. "She had to get out," the man sang, and the woman echoed him in a shout: "Get out!" Sigmone didn't usually like guitar songs, but this was okay.

"So y'all don't run around with those packs?" Sigmone asked finally.

"No, we have better things to do with our time," said Justin.

"Like sit in this freezing cold basement."

"Listen to music."

"Tell jokes."

"Do our nails."

"Tea parties."

"I get to watch Greg and Jenny make eyes at each other," said Justin. "That's awesome."

"Oh please." Jenny dismissed him with a gesture. "Says the world's biggest flirt."

"It's true, I am," Justin said, delighted. "You're very handsome, Sigmone. A little young for me."

"Uhhh," Sigmone said, and everyone laughed, even Sigmone. He didn't feel made fun of. He was being gently hazed, but by people who liked him.

"We choose not to participate in that mess," Greg said.

"The packs are fine," said Jenny. "They make the neighborhood work."

"We're a little more *civilized* down here." Justin raised his can of soda, pinkie in the air. "I have no interest in battling it out with animals."

"I'd kick your ass, for starters," said Greg.

"Oh, absolutely. I can't make any devastatingly cutting remarks," he confided, "when I'm a dog."

"You want something to drink?" Jenny asked, opening the cooler. "We have beer and soda."

"Do you have anything to eat? I'm starving."

All three made faces of sympathy. "Oh yeah, first time on four feet," Jenny said. "Sorry." She pulled a bag of Doritos out of her backpack.

"Thanks," he said, tearing the bag open and popping three chips into his mouth. They tasted amazing. He kept talking even as he chewed. "We're supposed to go to Burger King after we finish selling newspapers, but—what time is it?"

Greg looked at his watch. Sigmone decided not to wonder how he could wear a watch when he was a wolf. "Twenty to nine."

"Ah shit," said Sigmone, spraying Dorito crumbs. "I gotta find Joel and get back. That's my ride home."

"We can give you a ride," said Justin.

He had a license? Damn, they really were older than him. "No, that's cool, but I gotta find Joel, and I need to go back with my manager. He's responsible for all of us and I don't want him to worry."

The three looked at each other, shared some brain wave. "We'll come with you," Justin said. He turned off the music and picked up the boom box.

"It's fine. I'll be fine."

"We know, man," Greg said. "It's just, it's better if we all go together."

Sigmone decided not to push it, because he was relieved. "What do we do? Do we jump back out the window?"

Jenny opened a door to the backyard. "We *do* have opposable thumbs, Sigmone."

They walked up the driveway past the Olds on blocks. Belatedly, Sigmone realized this was the abandoned house that the neighbor had told him and Joel to avoid. "I think I remember the way to my grandpa's house from here," he said.

"I know it, too," Greg said. "My dad was in his pack." Jenny and Justin were a little ways in front of them, their heads together. Greg and Sigmone lagged behind. This was his first chance to really get a look at Greg, nearly as tall as Sigmone, light-skinned. His trench coat was weird, but he had big friendly eyes.

"So is there really a white pack and a black pack?" Sigmone asked.

"Hey, what else you expect in Milwaukee?" Greg said. "Even in a neighborhood where white people and black people live together, they still gotta separate themselves somehow."

"I am so sick of Milwaukee," said Justin from ahead. "I want to move to Minneapolis."

"Where do you live?" Greg asked Sigmone.

"Harambee," he replied. Justin and Jenny nodded politely but Greg raised his eyebrows.

"I've been there," he said. "That's cool."

The truth was that Sigmone was proud of his neighborhood, proud of his block. His mom and dad had drilled that into him, at least. Along with his grandfather, they'd been part of the protest group that had gotten Green Bay Avenue changed to Martin Luther King Drive. Yes, it was shabby compared to Whitefish Bay. Yes, he felt as alone there as he felt everywhere else, sometimes, when neighborhood kids sniffed at his white-kid school. But that was his home.

It had never really dawned on him that there might be something wrong with Milwaukee until he'd read Kareem's book. He'd known Kareem had played for the Bucks out of college; he used to watch games with his grandpa, when the last few players from that championship team were still kicking. What he hadn't known until he read the book was that Kareem didn't like Milwaukee. It was too cold; it was too white. He was Muslim and he didn't want to go out to taverns. He grew up in New York and went to college in LA. Suddenly here he was in the middle of nowhere dealing with—he said in the book—farmers! After six seasons Kareem had demanded a trade to the Lakers.

He'd never realized you could feel one way or another about Milwaukee. It was just the place he lived. Yes, he was loyal to Harambee, and he resented White Folks Bay. But not liking Milwaukee? You might as well not like air.

And now here was Justin, about as unlike Kareem as a person could be. But he, too, wanted out. As they walked, Sigmone thought, maybe for the first time ever: If he didn't live in Milwaukee, where would he live?

"What's in Minneapolis?" he asked.

"The Replacements," Justin said. "Prince. Any place that's got both of those, you gotta say, that's a real city, you know?"

Sigmone didn't know what he meant by the replacements, but he thought back to the book, to another line he'd underlined: "Milwaukee just wasn't a real city to me."

"It's okay here," Jenny said, blowing out smoke from a fresh cigarette. "These two can't wait to get out, but I like it. Lots of opportunities for a werewolf."

"You can't stay here," Justin said. "We're a pack. We all have to stick together forever. Too bad for you!"

"That is too bad, yeah," Jenny deadpanned.

"Oh please. Without me, how would you ever have any fun? You'd be studying chemistry twenty-four hours a day."

"Someone's gonna have to make money!"

"Sometimes," Greg said to Sigmone as they carried on, "it's like you wind 'em up and they just go and go."

"I like them," Sigmone said.

"Yeah, they're okay," said Greg. "It's good to have you here, though. Someone for me to talk to while they're just yappin' at each other."

"We do not *yap*," Justin said. "We *howl*." Then he struck a pose and, in an utterly human voice, said, "Aroo." Sigmone, too, got why that was funny. Sigmone, too, laughed at that. He didn't have to pretend. With these three unusual kids, he could just be. Now he just needed them not to figure out how young he was.

"What do you think they're doing now?" Joel asked.

"Probably marking lampposts," Kamika said. He could tell she was sick of him, but he couldn't stop himself from talking, asking questions, jiggling his knees—all the stuff that annoyed his dad. Everything bubbled up in him like a pot boiling over. He couldn't turn off the heat.

He was sitting at the kitchen table. She was washing dishes at the sink. She'd been really nice. She'd given him some potato chips and another Coke, which, honestly, probably wasn't helping things. Though she was trying not to show it, he could tell she was nervous—she kept looking up at the clock on the wall. Joel did, too. Pretty soon he had to get back to the van.

The other problem was that she was beautiful. He didn't know what to do about that. It seemed to demand some acknowledgment from him, but also, he felt as though he would drop dead if he said anything about it at all. He knew his stupid, fourteen-year-old words would crumple in the face of her perfection.

Last year Joel's science teacher, Miss Abraham, had been new to the school. She was younger than all the other teachers, and pretty, and a lot of the boys in class made fools out of themselves. "Who can wash out the pipettes for me?" she would ask, and boys would fall all over themselves to help. He'd overheard girls in the class complaining to one another about Miss Abraham's low-cut blouses, how she loved toying with the stupid boys. They sounded annoyed with her but also grudgingly admiring. Every once in a while she would look at him and ask him a question, and it would be like his brain turned off. He studied, he really did, but faced with Miss Abraham's blue eyes he couldn't remember a thing about the periodic table of elements.

At least he wasn't as bad as Danny Donoghue, who actually wrote Miss Abraham a love letter at the end of the year. Somehow word got around, because soon everyone knew about it, and then he *had* to go through with leaving it on her desk. No one saw what happened when she picked it up, but when Joel had asked Danny about it on the playground Danny had shoved him over.

Now, sitting in the kitchen with Kamika, he thought he could finally understand how a person could be driven to do something that insane by a woman's beauty. It made him nervous, and when he was nervous, he talked.

"Are they fighting?" he asked now. "With the . . . with the white wolves?"

"The *vargr*," she said.

"Are they at war with the vargrs?"

"It's not as simple as all that," said Kamika. She tore a paper towel and dried her hands. "The neighborhood is changing, so there's a lot of tension out there."

"And so the black people are fighting with the white people. I'm on your side, by the way," he said.

"They're not fighting. The wolves are why they're not fighting, mostly. You got some ideas about black people and white people, Joel." He could see her trying to work out how best to explain it, and he tried to look old enough for her to just *say* it, whatever it was. "Most of the time, everybody just deals with everybody else. One reason why is that most nights, the wolves are out."

"They keep an eye on things."

"Sure, yeah. But also in between them they sort of *act out* the everyday issues, and because they get settled there, everyone can relax in real life."

Joel wished he could relax. He was thinking about what she'd said, about his ideas about black and white. What were his ideas? He loved rap because it was cool, and because it made him cool, or sort of cool. He was the first one in his class with *Licensed to Ill*, and it had gotten kids over to his house all last year to listen to it and then, once they were there, to marvel at the gate, the studio, his room, all his shit. This year he could feel those friends fading away; the more time they spent

with him, the more irritating they seemed to find him, a response he
was used to from his dad. Being funny and outrageous helped a little.
He'd come up with the fart tape, which had gotten him through a bad
weekend at Boy Scout camp. Each time he said something outrageous,
he felt people drawn to him, but he had to keep doing wilder and
wilder things to keep their attention. Acting black was outrageous, at
first, but then a bunch of white kids started doing it. And he couldn't
help but notice that the four black students in his class didn't talk to
him. He guessed they didn't really care how down he pretended to be.
All they saw was a white kid trying on their blackness like an outfit.

"You're not a wolf," he said.

"No, that's right," she replied, sitting down. She rubbed her eyes.
"I'm not a wolf."

"Are you two married? If you had kids would they be, like, wolf
puppies?"

She looked at him levelly. "Not that it's any of your business, but
we're not married. I've been married. I don't need to do that again."

Joel guessed he wasn't going to get an answer to the second question.
But oh, oh, now she was sitting so close to him! She reached across
the table, took a potato chip, and ate it! And he could smell her, some
kind of stuff she must use on her hair or her skin. She smelled different from any person he'd ever met. He felt that sometime tonight,
he would get a chance to prove his quality to Kamika, and he hoped
that when the time came, he'd be able to find, deep within himself, a
man worthy of her love.

He sipped his Coke. His knee jiggled so hard it hit the underside
of the table at the exact moment the back door opened. He felt relieved, then resentful when he saw how she brightened at Augustin's
arrival, then alarmed. Where was Sigmone?

"He's not here?" Augustin asked at Kamika's look. "Damn." He looked the same as when he'd left, same clothes, same shoes. It was hard to believe Joel had seen him actually for real transform into a wolf. It hadn't been a long, gruesome transition like in the movies: hair growing, tail sprouting, mouth roaring in agony. One moment he and Sigmone had been in the front yard, lit by the spotlight like two actors on a stage, Sigmone yelling at his grandpa. Then Sigmone was a wolf, and then Augustin was a wolf. It happened in a blink—faster than a blink. It happened so effortlessly that for a moment Joel had felt fooled, like, oh, hadn't there always been wolves there?

"Don't you take those shoes off," Kamika said. "You gotta go back out there and find him."

Augustin shook his head and went to the refrigerator for a beer. "That's a bad idea," he said. "I go out alone, I'm liable to lose what we gained tonight."

"What did you gain?" Joel asked. "What happened?"

Augustin looked at him and raised his eyebrows at Kamika. "We tussled," he said. "Me and Owen. The pipefitters' union was slow-walking our guys' applications."

Kamika scoffed. "That's why you won't go out and find your grand-son? For a union application?"

"That's jobs for three brothers who need them. And anyway, he can handle himself. He ought to be able to, anyway." He sat down at the table and folded his arms. "That boy needs some room to explore."

"Talking about what that boy *needs*," Kamika said. "You barely know him."

Augustin stared at the table, not at her, not at Joel. "I know him," he murmured.

No one said anything. Joel thought of those kids at school, the ones who never talked to him. He thought how much he wanted to have a chance to make Kamika laugh, even just once. To show her he was more than what she thought he was.

He stood up. "I'll look for him," he said. "We need to get back to our manager soon."

Kamika turned her head from him to Augustin, Augustin to him, and then said the words he'd been dreaming of: "Fine. I'll go with you."

Look, he told himself as they walked out into the night. He knew she wasn't going to fall in love with him or something. He wasn't stupid. There was a huge cultural barrier between them, and also he was fourteen. But he felt an irresistible urge to do something, anything, with her. Yes, to get her away from Augustin, who was indisputably more impressive than him, even setting aside the part where he was a werewolf. But really just to be in her presence. To hear her voice.

"Should we call for him?" he asked. The street was quiet but felt maybe a little warmer than before. The snow was coming for sure.

"No, better not," she said. "We don't need to stir anything up."

He didn't see anything out there. No wolves, no monsters, no vampires, no nothing. The clouds obscured the moon (was it full tonight? He couldn't remember) but were themselves illuminated by the city light, casting an even glow over the street. He clutched the clipboard. The envelope with its single bill was in his coat pocket. His Swatch said it was a quarter to nine. He hoped they found Sigmone soon, but also, glancing at Kamika, he hoped they never found him.

From the shadows at the end of a dark driveway a wolf emerged, as big as Augustin. Or had it always been this man, in work boots and a Packers jacket? His face was stubbly with five o'clock shadow and he held one arm awkwardly at his side, as if it had been hurt. Even as a person, not a wolf, he intimidated Joel, because he could see that he was powerful, could feel Kamika tense up next to him. She tried to step in front of Joel, to get in between the man and him, but Joel sidestepped her and claimed his own spot in the conversation.

The man nodded. "Where's Augustin?"

"He's around."

The man tilted his head sideways and gave her a quizzical look. "I don't smell him," he said.

"Owen. What do you want?"

"There's a new one in your pack. Who is he?"

"It's not my pack."

He barely smiled. "Your *people*."

"Who Augustin runs around with is his business."

"And who are *you* running around with?" he asked, glancing at Joel. "Why's he with you?" Kamika took a step back. In the yards around them, in the dark corners, Joel sensed shadows moving silently, watching.

Joel took a deep breath. He stepped forward. "I'm selling subscriptions to the *Milwaukee Sentinel*," he said. "I see you're a Packer fan."

"Who's that down the street?" Greg asked.

"Ugh, that's our dad," Jenny said.

Sigmone squinted. "That's Joel!" He jogged a few steps forward and called his name. The three figures at the end of the block turned to look at them. Behind Joel, he could see, was Kamika, and he could tell, even from here, that the man in the Packers jacket was the wolf he'd seen his grandpa fighting.

As they approached, the man stepped away from Joel and Kamika and toward them. He gave a once-over to Sigmone, then turned to Justin and Jenny and talked to them as if the others weren't even there. "What do you think you're doing?" he asked.

"We're hanging out," Jenny said. "Jesus."

Justin laughed. "What is this, *West Side Story*?"

"Very funny."

"Hey, Sigmone!" Joel said, waving his clipboard. "I told you, man! That was *bad*, man!" He stopped short. "Are you all gonna eat me?"

"No, we're not gonna eat you," Sigmone said.

"Are they werewolves, too?" Joel asked.

Sigmone was instantly, painfully embarrassed to be known by this kid. "What exactly are you guys doing out here?" he asked.

"I was just telling this guy here about the commemorative plate," Joel said, cocking a thumb at Justin and Jenny's dad. Sigmone looked again. He felt the presence of other wolves, not far, and he clocked Joel standing in front of Kamika, and he thought, *Huh.*

"This is all going to end badly," the man said.

"It's only gonna end badly if y'all end it badly," said Greg.

"I'm not talking to you. I'm talking to my kids."

"He's right, though," Kamika said. "You all retreating to your own sides, fighting for the scraps. Instead of fighting the real enemy."

"Yeah, who's that?" the man said.

"Is it vampires?" Joel asked.

"The bosses!" Kamika said. "The people moving the factories away!"

"There's no vampires here," Jenny said. "They're all on the South Side."

A new voice chimed in, his grandpa's. "And what are we gonna do? March on Washington?" He emerged from behind a parked truck into the pool of light they all stood in. Sigmone had no idea how long he'd been nearby. He nodded at Justin and Jenny's dad, who nodded back.

"Boycotts!" Kamika said. "Community action! It's not rocket science!"

"Kamika went to school, unlike some of us factory men," Augustin said. "I think this is a discussion for another time. These kids need to get home."

The other man turned to his children. "We're only going if you come with us," Jenny said before he could speak.

The man turned back to Augustin. "I guess we'll continue this later," he said.

"Look forward to it."

"Dear Lord," Kamika said. "Just a bunch of mangy dogs fighting in the yard."

"Bye, Sigmone," Justin said, but his father was already ushering them up a driveway into the dark. Jenny gave a little wave, and then they were wolves, and then they were gone.

"We'll take Sigmone and Joel back to where they need to go," his grandpa said to Greg, his arms folded.

Greg looked at Sigmone and at Augustin. Sigmone wanted him to stay. He wanted to ask him how he got along with his white friends, how he got along in the world. He wanted to know more about the music they were listening to, and why his dad wasn't in the pack. But Greg ducked his head and said, "Okay, I understand." He looked up at Sigmone. "I'll see you around, maybe." And then he was running, four legs flying, a gray blur in the dark street.

"I'll never get tired of seeing that," Joel said happily.

Sometimes Sigmone had dreams where he was talking to a girl—sometimes a girl from his class, sometimes a girl from TV, sometimes (embarrassingly) his science teacher—and he could actually *talk* to her. He didn't clam up from shyness. He didn't stumble over his words. He didn't say anything stupid. He just told jokes, or complimented her, or asked her questions, and the girl responded. And they would talk awhile, and in the dream, the girl would draw close, smiling, and put her arms around him, and he could *feel* her up against him, and feel her warm breath on his face, and Lisa Bonet or his science teacher or whoever would lean in to kiss him, and just before their lips connected he would wake up.

This happened at least one night a week. And the instant he woke he would feel as miserable as a person could feel. The girl was gone. The dream was gone. He was alone in his too-small bed in his messy room. He could scramble all he wanted to remember what it felt like; he could even try to force himself back to sleep in the hopes of returning to it. But that kiss was never happening. Even worse, the kiss had never been real in the first place. He hadn't been smooth. He hadn't gotten someone to like him. It had been a dream.

Walking back toward Hampton with Joel and his grandpa and Kamika, he was reminded of this feeling, thinking of those older kids who had, for a brief moment, seemed like they could be his friends. It had been a powerful feeling, more powerful, even, than the feeling of running around with his grandfather's pack. But then he had woken up. He didn't have a car, he didn't have their phone numbers, he barely even knew where he was. Tonight he would climb into Kevin's van and return to his neighborhood. Tomorrow he'd get on the bus back to Whitefish Bay, awake and alone.

He could tell Joel had it bad for Kamika, the way he covered his awkwardness with chatter. The guy just didn't quit. He didn't think he could be friends with him, but he guessed he wouldn't mind seeing him around the halls. It might be good to have an eighth grader who knew his name, even a twerp like this one. At least he had that. At least they sold one subscription. At least he had Kamika's ten-dollar bill in his pocket. At least he was going to Burger King.

At least he'd found his grandpa, even if it was different from how he'd hoped it would be.

The tavern came into view, and the white van parked in front of it. There were two boys waiting there. Which ones were they again? As they got closer it looked like Mark and whatsisface, the quiet one. They both looked different, in some way Sigmone couldn't quite peg. Were they bigger somehow? Ryan—that was his name—he waved, obviously confused to see other adults walking with Sigmone and Joel. Then both boys' faces brightened with alarm, and they pointed behind Sigmone. He turned just in time to see the vargr leap at his grandpa.

In a snarl and a crunch of ice the two wolves rolled, tearing and snapping. And then there were more wolves, flooding out of the bushes and the backyards, both packs colliding here on busy Hampton Avenue, of all places. A car honked and screeched as two wolves rolled into the road. Another pair wrestled each other into a tree, which dropped a shower of ice onto their fur. It sounded like the inside of a pound. A terrified Mark and Ryan held themselves tight against the van, and Sigmone felt exhausted at the very idea of listening to Joel explaining everything to them.

A wolf rushed past them and Joel jumped in front of Kamika, took the hit, spun to the ground. Sigmone was so done with this shit. Done with these fucking wolves and this hero white kid and Hampton Heights. Sigmone grabbed Joel by the arm and dragged him toward the van. "My coat!" Joel said, showing Sigmone his ripped sleeve. "If he bit me, am I gonna turn into a wolf?"

"No," Sigmone said. "You'll turn black." He took a tiny bit of pleasure in the mixture of shock and fear that crossed Joel's face, felt bad about it, decided to think about it later.

You should expect trouble before you expect peace, Kareem had said in his book. Sigmone had underlined that, too. It had felt true then. It still felt true now. He reached into the wheel well where he'd seen Kevin hide the keys, and there they were. As the wolves fought in the yards and in the street, as cars honked and neighbors started coming out their front doors, as Kamika ducked into the tavern, he herded the other boys into the back of the van and climbed behind the wheel. "Look out for them back doors, they don't look sturdy," he said, and turned the key.

RYAN AND MARK

The deeper they went down 54th Street, the darker everything got. "This is like a horror movie," said Mark. "Can't you just see it? We're walking along, past a tree, then—BOO!"

Ryan jumped, despite himself. His mom didn't let him watch horror movies, not that he was going to admit that. "Should we figure out what we're supposed to say to people?" he asked.

Mark read the clipboard in a stupid-adult voice. "'Hello sir or ma'am, do you care what's going on in your community of NEIGHBORHOOD NAME?'" He snorted. "That's so corny. I'll take the lead. I'm good at stuff like this."

Ryan nodded, grateful. He was not good at stuff like this and admired those who were. He stopped and pointed. "I think this is the first house on the list."

The house at 4605 54th Street was a one-story cottage. The porch light was on, and they could see a figure moving behind the curtains in one of the windows. "Look, what are the odds we actually meet a murderer?" Mark said, finally.

"Pretty low," Ryan agreed.

"I'll take this one," Mark said, handing Ryan the empty envelope. "Let's fill this thing with cash and go eat a Whopper." He strode confidently up the walk, Ryan following, and rang the doorbell.

Inside the house the murmur of conversation stopped. Steps approached the door. When it opened, a tall black man looked out anxiously, then his expression settled as he saw the two teenagers. "I just got a minute, we're about to sit down to dinner," he said. "What are you boys selling?"

"Good evening to you, good sir," Mark said, and Ryan suppressed a laugh at his showman's flair. "My name's Mark, and I'm selling subscriptions to the *Milwaukee Sentinel*. You can get news about your community, your city, and your world, delivered to your door every morning. It costs just ten dollars for three months, or twenty-five dollars for a year." The man was nodding, looking for a way to interject, but the boy was a freight train. "Plus if you subscribe for a full year you get a special Green Bay Packers commemorative plate. Can I put you down for a subscription, sir?"

Finally there was a short silence. The man acknowledged Mark's feat with a nod, then said, "I think we already subscribe."

"No we don't!" a woman's voice said behind him. "You let it run out!"

"That's because we don't ever read it, honey," he said, still looking out the door at the boys.

"*You* never do. I like to read it in the morning with my eggs."

"Since when?"

"Since forever!"

"I'm out the door at five," he said, for the boys' benefit. "I don't usually get the chance to look at the news. So it's hardly worth the money."

"Well, sir," Ryan said, surprising himself, "what a wonderful Christmas gift it would be for your wife." Mark gave him a grin and a nod, like, *Nice one*. The man closed his eyes.

"That's right, Clyde," said the woman's voice. "What a wonderful *gift* that would be."

Eyes still closed, the man said, "I suppose I will subscribe for three months."

Mark wrote his name down on his clipboard. "You can pay now, or you can pay later," he said.

The man began to say something, but before he could, his wife called, "Pay now." With exquisite care, the man took two five-dollar bills from his wallet, opened the storm door, and handed the bills to Ryan, who tucked them into the envelope.

"Are they the paperboys?" his wife called.

"Are you the gentlemen who will deliver the papers?"

"No," said Ryan. "We have paper routes, but somewhere else. We're just out canvassing tonight."

"Aww, that's too bad," said his wife.

"Are you doing this whole block?" the man asked.

"Yeah," Mark answered. "You're our first customer."

"Your moms told you, like, don't go in strangers' houses and all that, right?" The man poked his head out the door for a moment, looked around the dark street. "It's a good neighborhood," he said quietly. "But I just want you to be careful. Hampton Heights can surprise you."

"It seems like a good neighborhood," said Ryan, who did not think that, exactly.

"It's magical, sort of," the man said dreamily. "I moved into this house just a few years ago and next thing you know I got a wife and a baby." As if summoned, the sound of a crying infant now came from inside the house. They heard the woman soothing the child, and the man looked back over his shoulder. "But there's magic and there's magic, you know what I mean?" he said.

His wife's voice rang out over the crying child. "What are you telling them boys?"

"Just telling them be careful out in those streets."

"Careful, yeah!" Her voice was closer now, but they still couldn't see her. "Otherwise you'll get et up." She and her husband both laughed.

"Well!" Mark said brightly, with the goal of bringing this weird conversation to an end. "Thanks for your subscription!"

Back on the sidewalk they marveled at their first sale. Maybe they could do this after all? It had been a lot easier than they'd expected, but then they'd had the man's wife doing most of their work for them. "Clyde Washington," Mark said, reading the man's name off his clipboard. They looked up at the house. The curtains were open now, and they saw Clyde Washington sitting at the table, a soup bowl in front of him, bringing the spoon to his lips. No one sat across from him.

Their optimism faded over the next half hour as they worked their way up the odd side of the block to Hampton, then back down the even side, and made no further sales. Some houses were clearly empty, their lights out and their driveways bare. They knocked anyway, just to cross them off the list. At one, their knock brought what sounded like an entire flock of wild birds to the door, screeching and flapping, and they bolted.

At other houses, the lights were on but no one was home, or at least no one willing to talk to them. Sometimes they saw a cracked blind or heard the TV inside. At one house, as they stood shivering at the door, Ryan identified the specific program the people inside were watching as *Who's the Boss?*

Mark, Ryan observed, was indefatigably cheerful. At every house where a resident did answer, he launched into his pitch with brio. He was changing it up a little, adapting his performance to the situation. He complimented housewives on their hair, beamed at screaming kids like a politician. At a house sporting an American flag, he delivered an aria about the First Amendment. Without evidence, he told another guy wearing a Marquette University sweatshirt that the commemorative plate honored the ten-year anniversary of that school's basketball championship. That guy came closest to actually buying a subscription, but balked when he asked what the plate looked like and Mark turned to Ryan expectantly, as if Ryan somehow was carrying an object that didn't, as far as he knew, exist. The man told them he'd think about it.

"Aw, man, we almost had that one," Mark said as they opened the gate and trudged down the sidewalk.

"Was I supposed to say something specific?" Ryan asked.

"Beats me," Mark said. "I was hoping you remembered the names of some of the guys on that team." Ryan, for whom sports had always made interactions with other boys a misery, who would rather read a book than pick up a ball, who was deeply grateful that in middle school recess was finally eliminated from the school day, who suffered stomachaches in gym class so frequently that his teacher had taken to just letting him sit in the bleachers, whose father had long since given up trying to get him to shoot some hoops or have a catch, did not remember the names of the guys on that team.

Mark, though, didn't seem mad. He grinned and chattered as they walked to the next house, speculating that this time he'd try a whole thing about the stock market. "My dad always looks at the stock prices in the business section," he said. "I bet that'll work."

Ryan wished he could share Mark's confidence. He was cold and hungry and discouraged by all the rejection. He could feel the warmth coming out of the houses when prospects opened the door, had once even smelled delicious cooking smells. But the doors always closed, and he should have brought a snack.

But he liked Mark. He liked that Mark never said anything about Ryan's height or weight or seemed to have any interest in making fun of him at all. He liked that Mark seemed to view each house they visited as an opportunity to showcase an all-new performance. At one house, he had even delivered the entire pitch in a British accent, like Monty Python. He liked that Mark, unlike anyone at Ryan's school, knew about Monty Python and enjoyed debating what their best sketch was.

He liked Mark's smile, and the brief moments when it vanished from his face and he became serious. But it was always hiding in there somewhere.

And he liked that despite Ryan mostly never having any clever things to say, Mark kept including him in his sales pitches, tossing him prompts—"Ryan, why don't you tell this beautiful lady how much a subscription costs?"—and nodding encouragingly while he stumbled his way through. It was too bad Mark went to a different school, lived in a different suburb; too bad that when the night was over, Ryan would be too shy to get his phone number and would surely never see him again.

They'd finished the block and were back where they started, across the street from the house of Clyde Washington, their only sale. Through the window, they could still see Clyde at the table, unmoving and alone. But then Ryan noticed, past Clyde's place, a house on the corner that they must have missed—a squat storybook cottage, nestled deep in the trees. "That must be 4601," Mark said.

"Is it on the list?"

Mark looked at his clipboard and blinked. "Oh yeah, there it is. My bad." He led them across the street.

In the gloom, they could see a dozen or more figures standing guard over the house: tall ones, short ones, lumpy ones, thin ones. Ryan said, "What are all those?"

"Statues," said a voice. Both boys jumped. "The witches make them."

A pair of the figures at the edge of the property moved and revealed themselves as kids, standing with their hands in their pockets. Oh man, Ryan thought, slipping the envelope with the ten dollars into his coat. As if they needed this. The kids looked tough. One was black and one was white. The bigger kid, the white one, wore a convincing-looking leather jacket and had the hint of a mustache. The smaller one, about Ryan's height, wore a rainbow-colored vest and a White Sox hat. Here in Milwaukee, the hint of a connection to Chicago suggested you might be a very bad kid indeed.

Ryan could tell that Mark had as little interest as he did in mixing it up with these kids, in this neighborhood, on this night. Mark was taller than Ryan—that is to say, average height for a thirteen-year-old—but nothing about him suggested he welcomed a fight. He shoved his hands in his pockets and said, "What witches?"

"You're not from around here, are you?" asked the big one.

"No," said Mark. *Don't say you're from Glendale*, Ryan thought. "We're from another part of town." He looked at Ryan, and this time the imperative to add something was serious, and Ryan took it seriously.

"We're selling newspaper subscriptions," he said, trying to make his voice as confident as possible. "Our boss drove us here." He waved in the direction he believed the van to be, hoping to convey that the boss could, at any moment, show up.

"The witches live there," the smaller kid said, pointing at the little stone house in the shadows of the wood. "They make all those statues. There's two of them."

"What do you mean they're witches?" Mark asked.

Both kids shrugged in unison. "Everyone knows it," said the bigger one. "If they trap you in their house, you never come out again."

"And that happened? Like, to someone you know?"

The boys shrugged again. "Everyone knows it," the bigger one repeated.

"There's always dead animals," the smaller kid said. "I see those old ladies, they're picking weeds and plants and shit, and there'll be a dead fox right there."

"One of 'em smokes a pipe," added the bigger kid.

"Have you ever seen them, like, stirring a cauldron?" Mark asked.

Ryan felt himself smile, though he tried to hide it. "Do they fly around on broomsticks?" he said.

"Do they wear pointy hats?"

The kid in the leather jacket took one step closer to them, just to remind them how big he was. "That's funny," he said. "You guys are funny."

"No, they don't fly on no broomsticks," the smaller kid said. "Don't be stupid."

"They drive a pickup truck," said the bigger kid.

"But look at those statues."

Mark and Ryan looked. The yard was crowded with them. A trio of small, ghostly shapes carved from wood gathered in a triangle. Their tiny black eyes looked out at the world. A stone fish walking on two feet peeked out from behind a tree. Two creatures with snakes for hair sat on a cement bench, as if waiting for the bus. Closest to them was a stone dinosaur taller than any of the kids, blue painted rocks for eyes, leaning forward to menace the sidewalk, its mouth in a frozen roar. The big kid opened his mouth wide in imitation. "Garrrrrr," he said. His teeth were covered in braces.

"You gonna sell them a magazine subscription?" the shorter kid asked.

"It's the newspaper," Mark said. "And they're on our list."

"Well, that's gonna be death of a salesman then, boy," the kid said, and he and the bigger kid slapped five, laughing.

Ryan did not at all want to walk through those statues, with their blank, staring eyes. He didn't want to knock on the door and meet the old women who made them, who plucked weeds from corpses, who lived in a house overgrown by vines and covered in dead leaves and dirty snow. But Mark rolled his eyes at the other boys and said,

"They're being gay," and then turned to Ryan and beckoned him forward. "Come on, Ryan."

Ryan couldn't help admiring Mark's bravery, even as he heard the word he used, a word that had always in his experience preceded some other, even worse taunt. But he followed him to the house's front walk, which was flanked by two huge heads, like those statues on Easter Island. Behind them, the boys chuckled and muttered to each other. Somewhere in the distance, a group of dogs howled.

"I bet those old ladies need newspaper for, like, papier-mâché or whatever," Ryan suggested.

"Hell yeah," Mark said. They took a few steps up the walk and then Mark turned back to the kids. "If these ladies are so scary," he called, "why are you here?"

The boys stared at them for a long moment. Finally, the taller one spoke.

"We were waiting for you," he said.

The house, on a corner lot, was set much farther back than the others on the block, and the path wound its way through the yard. Even as they walked toward it, the little house seemed to recede into the dark trees, its porch light nearly dancing in the gloom. The statues seemed to be following him with their eyes, so Ryan tried to narrow his focus to Mark in front of him, the house in front of Mark.

The house.

It was one story plus an attic, and it was covered in creatures.

The front porch roof sported a bright-red fish skeleton—maybe meant to be a whale, it was so big. Holding up the screened porch were two wooden columns; carved into each were snakes and centipedes, making their way up the smooth surface in relief. There was a big picture window to the left of the door; in the bushes, a gaggle of toddler-size figures gathered, curiously looking up and into the window.

It was taking them so long to get to the house. The sounds of the neighborhood had fallen away and now all Ryan heard was the crunching of their feet on the icy path. The trees towered over them, bare branches like arms, evergreens like a blanket. The whole thing, in Ryan's opinion, was way scarier than it needed to be.

Mark finally reached the porch door and rang the doorbell. Ryan expected one of those haunted-house *BONG BONG*s, but it chimed just like his doorbell.

"Maybe no one's home," Ryan said.

"They're home."

Indeed, the inner door opened with a creak, and through the dirty screen the boys saw a tall, heavyset woman flip on the porch light and make her way toward the door. She stepped silently in fuzzy slippers and wore a flowered dress. When she opened the door, she said in a cheerful voice, "Hello there! How can I help you two?"

Her graying hair was up in a bun and she wore reading glasses on a chain around her neck. Her face was kind. Ryan never knew how old grown-ups actually were—he had once enraged his uncle's girlfriend by guessing she was fifty—but the woman at the door looked to be his grandparents' age, or maybe a little older. She didn't look like a witch.

"Hello there!" Mark echoed. His carnival-barker voice was back, only slightly diminished by nervousness. "I'm Mark, and this is Ryan."

Ryan never knew what possessed him, but he blurted, "We're traveling salesmen!"

The woman laughed, a big, happy laugh. Mark looked back at Ryan, grinning. Ryan felt something take flight inside him.

"My goodness," the woman said. "Look at you two. What are you selling? Encyclopedias?"

"Ma'am, we're selling something better than encyclopedias," said Mark. Last year Ryan's choir teacher had showed the class *The Music Man*, and this was what that was like. "Encyclopedias, what do they contain? The past. Ancient Sumeria and the like. But a woman like you, you want to know what's happening *right now*. You need *the newspaper*. We're offering subscriptions to the *Milwaukee Sentinel*. You can get today's news delivered to your door every morning, plus business, entertainment, sports—are you a sports person?—and the funny pages, for just ten dollars for three months. But I recommend you subscribe for the whole year, just twenty-five dollars. That way for all of 1988 you'll know what's going on in the, uh"—here Mark spread his arms expansively and looked around, only to see, in the yard next to them, a second woman.

She had come around the house, it seemed, without them noticing. She was petite, brown-skinned, dressed in a suit, with glasses perched on her nose. She'd gathered branches and held them under one arm. She was giving them a teacher's look.

". . . what's going on in the world?" Mark finished, a little weakly.

The woman on the porch clapped her hands. "Millie, look at this. We've got a talker."

"We do," the woman in the yard said.

The first woman reached out her hand, every finger bearing a sparkling ring, and draped it over Mark's shoulder. She leaned close and looked him right in the eye. "I'm a talker, too." With a brilliant smile, she added, "It's awfully cold out here. Won't you come in and tell us more?"

Ryan opened his mouth to say, "We're not allowed," but then Mark turned toward him, his face gleaming with joy. It was as if going into this old lady's house was his dream coming true. Mark followed the woman onto the porch and through the front door.

Ryan's feet felt glued to the ground. What had just happened? What was he supposed to do? At the second woman's feet he saw, creeping from the ground that he could have sworn was frozen solid, a tiny green shoot. At its end a small flower opened, blue as a sky.

The woman followed his gaze and grunted. "No, no," she grumbled, stooping down, still holding the kindling. She reached out with her other hand, took hold of the flower, and yanked it from the ground. She slipped it into her mouth and chewed. "We have warm apple cider," she said to Ryan, standing back up. "Children like that." Her face suggested she herself couldn't imagine.

Still Ryan didn't move. Finally the woman opened the screen door and stepped into the porch. "Please yourself," she said. "But he will need you."

Ryan took a step forward, another step. The statues watched him follow her through the screen door and into the warm house. Out on the sidewalk, the other boys were long gone.

Now Mark and Ryan were sitting together on a green leather couch in the ladies' living room. "I don't know what happened," Mark whispered. "I just was there and then I was here."

"We can go," Ryan said. The ladies were clinking and clanking in the kitchen and not checking on them at all. The door was right behind them.

Mark shook his head. "We're here now." He set the clipboard on his lap and drummed a little *rat-a-tat-tat* with his fingers.

The décor didn't at all match Ryan's idea of what two old ladies would put in their living room. His grandma's house was filled with flowery armchairs and Precious Moments. This living room looked—well, he was no interior designer, but it looked modern. He saw a low, round coffee table, and sleek gray chairs, and a rug that looked like it belonged on *The Jetsons*. Up on the walls were framed drawings of the forest, a river, a little house, the lady who'd answered the door.

The women were back in the room. "We haven't introduced ourselves," said the one in the dress, bearing a tray laden with steaming mugs. "I'm Vincel. And she"—she nodded over at the other woman, who was setting a plate of cookies on the coffee table—"is Millie."

"Millicent," the other woman said with a scowl.

"Everyone calls her Millie," Vincel said cheerily.

"What kind of cookies are those?" Ryan asked.

"Lebkuchen," Millie said.

"Gingerbread," Vincel explained. Her voice was like the bell choir at Ryan's church, chiming and chiming. "And here's warm apple cider, as promised." She set a mug in front of each of the boys. On Mark's mug, Ryan recognized the logo of a bookshop he'd visited on the east side. Ryan's read FAIR HOUSING NOW. He warmed his hands near the mug but for now didn't pick it up.

Mark, too, didn't take anything, and after a moment Vincel laughed. "Oh dear, those boys outside have told you stories, haven't they?" She put up her hands and opened her mouth wide as a dinosaur's, and looked for a moment so much like the big kid on the sidewalk that Ryan didn't even know what to do.

"We're not going to eat you," said Millie, unconvincingly.

"We just want to *feed* you!" said Vincel.

"Where do those statues come from?" Ryan asked.

"We make them, of course," said Vincel. "From wood and stone, not from children. Now, you poor boys, you're cold and hungry. Have a bite and we'll talk about your newspaper."

Ryan picked up his mug. The cider smelled delicious, like cinnamon and evergreen. He brought the mug close to his face and let the steam touch him. Mark, next to him, had picked up a cookie and had broken off a piece. He held it up to the light as if, by staring at it closely, he might identify the danger.

Their eyes met. Ryan saw Mark shrug the tiniest shrug and raise one eyebrow. He was grinning again. Ryan grinned, too. How likely was it, really, that these two random old ladies were planning on poisoning them? And how cold and hungry were they? And how grateful, after house after house of rejection, to be welcomed into this warm and comfortable place? To be clucked over by these two women who even now smiled kindly at them from their matching chairs? (Well, Vincel smiled. Millie's face showed more of a grimace, as if smiling was painful but she was making the effort.)

They nodded to each other and, at the same time that Mark popped the cookie into his mouth, Ryan brought the cider to his lips. It was so warm, the perfect temperature, and as it touched his tongue he felt his whole body relax, flooded with comfort. He was safe here. He saw Mark's eyes close with pleasure at the taste of the cookie and he knew he felt the exact same way.

"You boys are in cahoots," Vincel said happily. "I can tell."

"Yeah," Mark said, still chewing, eyes still closed. "We're a team."

They both sank back into the couch. Ryan held the mug carefully in both hands, close to his chin, so he wouldn't spill. He took another sip of the cider and this time really tasted it: the apples picked from an orchard just a few miles from here, the steel squeeze of the press. A winter orange. Spices from the other side of the world. He saw the bark painstakingly stripped from a cinnamon branch by brown hands. He saw an ocean of cloves drying on reed mats in the sun. The cider swirled in a red enamel pot over a low flame.

Next to him, Mark took another bite.

Vincel's eyes were bright. "I thought," she said, "you might like to hear the story of how we met."

"It is a tale of woe," said Millie.

Vincel chuckled. "I prefer to think of it as a story where we *overcome* the woe, dear Millie."

"Speak for yourself, dear Vincel."

"Let me assure you," Vincel said, "that you will be safe for as long as you wish to stay."

Her voice was far away. Ryan could feel his arm pressed against Mark's. He felt inexpressibly happy, at home in this weird place, for once at home in his disobedient body. The women told him a story, and he listened.

Deep in the forest, in the valley of the river that runs uphill, past the clearing where no sunlight shines, there once was a humble house of logs and thatch. In that house lived a mother, poor but hardworking, and her daughter. As a girl, the daughter did not understand all that they lacked, but as she turned into a young woman, she came to know how tirelessly her mother labored to provide for them and did all she could to help. She grew tall and strong, and soon could spin yarn from a wheel, tend to a sick animal, or repair a cart.

The house was steadfast against the cold wind of winter that blew through the valley but in the warm summers, after a long day of gathering food and mending clothing, the daughter sometimes felt how small and stuffy the house could be. On those evenings she would open the windows wide, light a candle to keep the mosquitoes away, and listen to the buzz and rustle of the night.

It was because of those open windows that, one night, she heard a faraway voice singing a song she could almost make out. The voice was strong and deep, a woman's voice, and as it grew nearer the little house in the forest she at last recognized the song, one that, she recalled, her mother had sung to her when she was small.

I will remember
The black of your hair,
The green of your eyes,
The scent in the air.

I will remember
The wine on our tongue,
The candies and pies,
How it felt to be young.

I will remember
The touch of your hand,
Every sunrise,
This gold gimmel band.

The girl's mother was asleep in her bed, and the daughter had no desire to wake her, but nonetheless she found herself singing along to the song she knew so well, joining her voice to the voice in the forest in sweet and lilting unison:

And if you remember the love that we share
Then find me again as the bird finds its nest.
For you are my home and my darling so rare
This gimmel ring shared with the one I love best.

As the last word faded away, a woman stumbled out of the forest. She was small and handsome, with dark hair and olive skin. She appeared even poorer than the daughter's family, carrying over her shoulder a bundle that looked to contain little more than a cookpot. She bowed to the daughter. "My queen," the woman said.

"I am no queen," the girl said, laughing.

"Yet you sit up there in your window, as elegant as a royal portrait." The woman set down her bundle, looked around, and sat upon the ground. The daughter was grateful to see that the woman took care to avoid sitting on any of the sprouting bean shoots that were the garden's treasure.

The woman was a wandering artist. She traveled from town to town, sketching those she encountered and living off what she could scrounge, what she could gather, and what those who appreciated her drawings might give her. "And what I steal," she added. "Have you ever left a loaf of bread cooling on your windowsill, then to find it gone, with only the crumbs left over? That was me."

"We rarely have flour for bread," the daughter said. "I don't think that's ever happened to us."

"Could have been an egg," the woman allowed. "Some people leave those out."

"On the windowsill?" said the daughter. "Wouldn't it roll off?"

"Not if I steal it first!" declared the traveler.

The daughter laughed. Tired as she was, she still had fuel in her heart for whimsy. In her poor mother's heart such fuel had long since burned away. Though the mother was never less than kind, she rarely saw delight in the world, and though her daughter could still clap her hands like a child the mother rarely had time for play.

The girl and the traveler talked long into the night. The daughter revealed secrets she'd never told her own dear mother. The woman spoke of the great world outside the forest and all the marvelous people it contained. And the girl's mother, though she might most nights be awakened by any owl's call or cracking branch, slept soundly and woke in the morning refreshed and not a little puzzled by her daughter's exhaustion.

"Why do you sleep so late?" asked the mother, as the sun streamed into the garden and through the open window. "It is the first day of spring, and the weather is fair."

The girl stirred and smiled into her hand. Her long hair was a tangle of knots. At the darkest, deepest part of the night, the moment when the clouds parted to reveal the cold twinkling stars, the traveler had taken up her bundle and walked away—but she had left the daughter a honeycomb and promised to return on the first night of autumn, when her travels would again take her through the forest. In her bed, before she slept, she had felt the honeycomb's weight in her hand and then eaten it whole.

Spring and summer went by in a flurry of planting, cooking, trips to market, and trips back home. The daughter kept her secret but felt toward her mother more tender than ever. Once, her mother, too, had met someone who must have made her feel as the daughter did now—her own father, gone from their lives so long that her mother never even spoke of him. As her mother fed the chickens or tended the beans, her mouth a line as straight as an oxcart's track, the daughter watched her work, and loved her all the more.

And in the spot in the garden where the woman had sat, in the patch of earth between the rows of beans, wildflowers grew. Her mother raised her eyebrows at the riot of purples and yellows but let them bloom. The bees they attracted were good for the rest of her vegetables. In the late afternoon, before she started helping her mother make the evening meal, the daughter would watch the bees land on the flowers, exploring them, and she'd remember what it had felt like, late that night, when she'd sunk her thumb deep into the honeycomb.

On the first night of the fall, the daughter plaited her hair and waited by the window long after her mother fell asleep. The air was cool, and as the fire dwindled in the hearth it became cooler still. The daughter felt older than she had ever felt before, and nervous for the traveler's return, and more nervous still that the traveler might not come at all. Her hand rested in her apron pocket, running her finger along the gift nestled within.

She grew sleepy; she grew sad. But then from the depths of the moonless night she heard the song she'd spent the summer humming to herself:

I will remember
The black of your hair,
The green of your eyes,
The scent in the air.

From her window the young woman joined the song. The traveler emerged from the darkness. Her trousers and shirt were even more worn than before. She sported a long scrape down the dark skin of her cheek. But she smiled to see the daughter, smiled as they finished the song together. The traveler stood astride the wildflowers and beamed up at the daughter on her throne.

"The honeycomb was wonderful," the daughter said. "Now I've a gift for you." From her pocket she pulled a single egg and placed it carefully upon the windowsill. The egg balanced for a moment, then rolled toward the edge and fell out the window—

—but the traveler stepped forward, reached out a hand, and caught it. She stood so close that the daughter could smell the road upon her. The traveler held up the egg. "Thank you," she said. "But you were right, it did not stay upon the sill."

The daughter took another boiled egg from her pocket and tapped it on the sill, just hard enough to flatten the bottom of its shell. When she took her hand away the egg stood at attention on the narrow sill. The woman laughed, tapped her own egg, and left it with its mate. Then she gently touched the daughter's soft hand with her own calloused fingers.

At the darkest part of the night, as the traveler prepared to depart, the daughter said, "I do not wish to keep this secret."

"What do you mean?" asked the woman.

"I want my mother to know you," the daughter said. "I want her to understand how I love you." She looked upon the traveler, frightened that she might reject this request, that she'd declare she was never coming back.

But the woman thought for only a moment before she said, "That is what I want, too." She told the girl that she would once again return when her travels took her back through the forest. "On the first night of spring," she said, "return to this window, and bring your mother with you. I would meet her, and share a gift, and ask for a gift from her in return." Then she took her egg and, peeling it, disappeared into the shadows.

Ryan stirred. Gentle morning light came through the windows of the house. Mark held out a glass of water and Ryan took it and drank so deeply that a little spilled out onto his sweater. He saw his coat and Mark's, hanging from hooks by the door.

"They *are* witches," Mark said. Ryan heard the women in another room, murmuring and moving around. A sewing machine hummed.

"They enchanted us," Ryan said. "The cookies. The cider."

Mark sighed. "I wish I had more of the cookies right now."

Ryan, brave somehow, put his hand on Mark's shoulder. Mark's gaze focused on him. "Do you want to go home?" Ryan asked.

"I know I should," said Mark. "But I want to stay and hear the rest of the story."

When the women returned with breakfast, the boys were asleep, slumped against each other on the green leather couch. Vincel tutted. Millie observed with annoyance that they hadn't used a coaster on the coffee table, and now there was a ring. The women lifted them effortlessly, carried them to the guest bedroom, tucked them under the covers. Millie reached up and closed the drapes.

Through the fall the young woman and her mother harvested the crops from the small field they oversaw, and stored fruit and meat, and sold

crafts at the market. They protected the chickens from foxes and re-
paired the spots in the walls of the little house where the wind blew
through. During the winter they sat by the fire and sewed and whittled
as the snow fell silently outside. More than once the daughter thought
of her traveler and the thin shirt she wore. How would she remain
warm through the long, dark season?

The snow melted, as it always does, and trees began to bud, as they
always do. The young woman felt impatient, stuck, as she never had
before. She loved her mother but for the first time in her life wondered
what it was her mother was raising her to do. Was she never to leave
the little house in the forest? Was she ever to make her own way in
the world that her traveler had described? On their trips to the market
she began asking after the provenance of each ingredient they bought
or bartered for. The round cheese from a cave on the other side of the
mountain; the white wine from the great vineyards on the other side
of the wide river; the three precious cardamom pods that came on a
ship from the subcontinent. And what does the wind sound like in
the cave? she asked. How does the grape taste when plucked from the
vine? What does the sailor feel when the ship makes its way to open sea
and the land disappears over the horizon?

And still spring approached, and still the daughter had not told
her mother about the traveler of her heart.

As the first day of spring neared, the daughter did not fear that
the traveler would not return, for she trusted in their love. And just in
case, she had placed an enchantment on that boiled egg, so that when
the traveler had eaten it the night she walked away, she would be com-
pelled to return.

But she wondered how best to tell her mother about the person
who, she trusted, was approaching, as sure as warm weather. She
knew she wanted her mother to know, wanted her mother to meet the
traveler, but she feared her mother's response. Would she scorn her

daughter for falling in love so quickly, with someone whose prospects were so poor? Would she feel rejected or betrayed? Or worst of all, she could imagine her mother feeling nothing—being so far removed from the experience of first love, so worn down by the toil required by the little house, that she could not share the joy her daughter felt bursting through her every day.

The final morning of winter was drizzly and dark. The young woman awoke early, stoked the fire, and milked the cow, and collected the eggs, and plucked a single leaf off the sage that had survived the cold. Inside she hung up her damp cloak and set to cracking eggs and mixing them with a splash of milk. She cooked them into an omelet and sprinkled the omelet with sage and salt and the tiniest bit of the cheese from the cave. (The sound of the wind in the cave, she had learned, was like a mouth singing a mournful song, but one that has no beginning and no end.) She brought the omelet to her mother in her bed.

The omelet was small and delicious. The mother, warmed to see her daughter so busy and so happy, gave her the last bite. After the daughter swallowed, she said, "Mother, tonight we will have a visitor."

The mother listened carefully to what her daughter told her. She said, "And you are certain that you love her?"

"Yes." She gave a determined nod, and in the firelight the mother saw a glimpse of the headstrong little girl she once had been.

"My child has been my greatest joy," the mother said. "That is a dear sacrifice to make. I could not have lived without a child. Will you be able to?"

"I don't know," said the daughter.

The mother rose from her bed. The young woman looked on anxiously. The mother laid a hand on her daughter's cheek and said, "We have a lot of work to do today, to welcome a guest into our home tonight."

Before the daughter's disbelieving eyes, her mother set about making the shabby little cottage a place of magic and beauty. With cleverness and care the mother transformed what little they had and what little she could find into a setting fit for a princess of the forest. She searched the woods around their house for daffodils, for spring violets, for evergreen boughs and bright green leaves. She decorated their little square table and placed cushions upon the seats of the chairs. And after dinner she used the last of their molasses to make a sweet cake, round and flat, for the lovers to eat.

Another night had gone by. Or was it more? Ryan wasn't hungry anymore, didn't need anything but to know what would happen next in the story. Vincel and Millie sat in their chairs, and the fireplace crackled, and the room filled with words.

"The mother," he heard Mark say. Their hands were clasped together on the couch. "Will she be okay?"

"That is what the story will tell," Vincel replied. That afternoon the boys squeezed into the cab of the pickup truck and rode to Menards, where they wandered the aisles as if in a dream. Ryan pushed the cart. Millie filled it with sidewalk salt and topsoil.

"Are we out of varnish?" Vincel asked.

"Yes, Vincel, you used the last of it on that beautiful statue of a bear cub."

"Oh, yes, how silly of me."

At the register, the saleswoman said, "Your boys are so well behaved."

"They're not our boys," growled Millie. "Do you sell deodorant?"

In the truck on the way home, Ryan asked, "Do I have a mother?"

"Yes, my duck, you do, you do," Vincel replied. "She would miss you very much, as the mother in the story knows she will miss her child." And though Ryan knew it was true it didn't alarm him. The feeling lived somewhere deep underneath, in a place where he could see it but not feel it, no matter how he reached.

"I bet she wouldn't miss your stink, though," Millie said. "Why did we have to get teenagers this time?" The next morning Millie made both boys take a bath. They sat back to back and scrubbed themselves, murmuring to each other about the house in the woods where the singing girl lived.

Late that night the young woman and her mother waited together in the window. The weather had turned. It was a calm, dry evening, and in the garden three lanterns flickered invitingly. The daughter held her mother's hand as, from the woods, they heard the singer sing:

> *I will remember*
> *The wine on our tongue,*
> *The candies and pies,*
> *How it felt to be young.*

This time the daughter and her mother joined in, and the traveler appeared in the lanterns' light, her mouth, too, open in song. The traveler's cloak was torn and her pants ripped at the ankle. She seemed even thinner than before, and her hair was longer and messier. She looked more than ever a creature of the woods, fierce and dangerous. But she was beautiful even still, and the mother saw the adoration for her daughter in her face and loved the traveler, too.

"Come into our home," the mother said when the singing had ended. "Please stay the night."

Inside the cozy and beautiful house, the traveler told mother and daughter of her journeys across borders. The warmth of the fire and the wine bloomed in her cheeks as she spoke of the long swamps in the north, of the castle on the wall where every year she drew a portrait of a king, only to find that in a year's time there was always a new king to draw. She told them of a harbor on the seashore visited by a selkie, of the villages where the rules were made by wolves, and of the spectral pickpockets who roamed the great cities on the rivers.

"And where did you come from?" asked the mother. "Who are your people?"

"Ah, that is not a tale worth telling," demurred the traveler, but the mother insisted. Finally she said that her parents had given her up to the church in her infancy, but that the fathers had treated her ill and the sisters, resentful, looked the other way. "I was neither boy nor girl to them, valued only for what they could take from me, and so on my tenth birthday I ran away." She looked away and the firelight played on a tear wending its way down her cheek. The daughter put out a hand, stopped short, looked at her mother. When her mother nodded, the daughter stroked the traveler's hair.

"Have you been a traveler ever since?" asked the mother.

"I have," she said. "Fifteen years it has been, and I have had hard journeys and easy ones, but never have I longed to return to a place as I have to this house."

The mother retired to the bedroom and let the lovers share the molasses cake, drizzled with the morning's cream. As she sat on the edge of her bed, she thought of the tenderness of her daughter's touch at that moment. Was the traveler merely telling a tale? Was the tear real? She could only trust her daughter, and her daughter's judgment, she supposed.

Her daughter called from the other room, her voice filled with joy. The mother got up from the bed—oh, how it hurt to stand—and stepped into the doorway. The traveler was holding up a drawing.

"It is a gift for you," the traveler said. "I drew your daughter over and over in the months since I saw her last, and taught my memory to keep her face close to the surface. But now that I see the drawing here in this house, I see that it looks like her and also does not; it also looks like you."

The mother took the drawing in her hand and held it up to the firelight. Indeed, it did resemble the face that stared back at her from the bucket of water drawn from the well. And it resembled the daughter's face, beaming now at her mother, her arm linked through the traveler's.

"Thank you for this gift," the mother said, and she had to fight to control her voice, which wished to fly away out of her throat, like a bird. "I will treasure this portrait when my daughter is gone from here, journeying with you on the road. For is there a question you wish to ask me, to accompany this gift?"

The traveler nodded. The young woman's face became grave, and the mother held back a cry of pain at her sudden seriousness, at the way she was listening so hard and trying desperately to remember every second of this visit. "I do wish to ask for your daughter's hand," the traveler said.

"Her hand is hers to give," said the mother. "Not mine."

"I give it," said the daughter.

"I am grateful to you both," said the traveler. "But for now you, madam, will retain both your daughter and this portrait, for I must travel six months more before I can return and we can be wed." She explained that she needed to make herself a prospect worthy of her bride, to earn enough money to support them in their first years together. "I don't even own a suit of clothes suitable for a wedding," she said. "But when I return, at the end of summer, I shall have that, and more besides."

The daughter was crestfallen, but nodded. The mother could hardly speak for joy, though she knew enough to hide her delight as she had hidden her sorrow. Instead, she simply said, "That is wise, traveler. I am grateful that you are preparing so diligently for your life together."

The daughter sat up with resolve. She said, "Mother, it will be wonderful to share this final summer together, and to prepare the house and garden for my departure."

In the morning, the traveler cleaned the spot before the fire where she had spent the night. She gathered her bundle and gratefully accepted a morning meal from the mother. Before she left, she pulled something shining from her pocket and held it up to the sunlight. It was a gimmel ring, two circles of gold that locked together at a hinge. She unfastened the joint and handed a ring to the daughter. The traveler said, "We both wear them, so we remain in each other's thoughts, though I will be far away."

The young woman, trembling, slipped her ring on. The traveler did, too. As she walked away, the mother and daughter saw the sun glint off her hand, just before she stepped into shadow.

Never had the mother felt a summer go by so fast as that one, when she and her daughter worked every day from sunup to sundown. There was so much to do, to prepare the house for a time without the daughter. Only occasionally would the mother see her daughter resting in a chair, or under a tree, one hand dreamily twisting the ring around her finger.

Never had the daughter felt a summer go by so slowly. Every task took an eternity to complete, and every day was filled with so many tasks, to prepare her mother for her departure. Her mother, too, worked tirelessly, she knew, and the daughter saw her grow thinner as the summer went on, though the harvest was good and their cookpot was full. Only occasionally would the daughter see her mother take a moment away from her work and rest leaning on the hearth, looking at the portrait the traveler had drawn in its place over the table.

And then, on the hottest day of the summer, the daughter came home with a basket full of berries to find her mother, flushed and panting, lying in the garden. Her head rested on the bed of wildflowers. Her legs crushed a row of their best beans.

Some mornings Ryan woke while Mark still slept. Those mornings he always felt as though he was swimming up from a deep, deep place, and finally surfacing in a calm sea. He lay in bed, Mark breathing deeply beside him, and looked at the shadows of the leaves on the drapes in their room, idly flickering in the springtime sun. When he got up and moved, quiet as he could, to the kitchen, he found that Vincel and Millie were always up, cooking or carving or drawing. He didn't think they ever slept. Why would they need to?

He felt, on these mornings, some sense that there was something he didn't quite understand. He would ask the women, where did he come from? Why didn't he go to school? Did he not have a family? And the women would give him honest answers: He knocked on their door one night. He didn't go to school because it did not serve the women's aims for the boys to do so. He had a family, and so did Mark, and if he was truly gone, they would miss him so. But he was not truly gone. "You are here and not here," said Vincel. "You are safe, so long as you wish to stay. Do you want to leave?" And he always said no.

On this morning Vincel and Millie were in the living room. "You're restless," Millie said. She sat on an ottoman, making lines in a sketchbook.

He sat on the couch and picked up the *Milwaukee Sentinel*. It was May, the newspaper said. "What happens in the world while we are here?" he asked.

"Oh, what always happens in the world, my duck," said Vincel.

"People fight for a good life, a meaningful life, for the ones they love. And the forces arrayed against them always seem daunting."

"Who do you fight?"

"Pssh, no one," Vincel said. "We're long beyond that."

"That's not true," Millie said sharply. "We've always fought." In the 1960s, she said, they marched every day for a year for fair housing in Milwaukee. "And even now," she said, pointing to the newspaper, with its photo of protesters and police. "Even now we fight how we can."

"Yes, she's right," Vincel said. "I apologize, Millie. We're making a world for you, now, and for Mark. For you love each other, don't you?"

"Yes," said Ryan.

Millie stood up and walked to the kitchen. "You're growing like weeds," she complained. "How are we supposed to keep you dressed?"

Ryan looked down. It was true that finally, at long last, he was getting taller, and his ankles were now exposed to the air. He wouldn't say he was skinny but he wasn't shaped like a bowling ball anymore.

"Ah, it's warm already," said Vincel. "These boys need summer clothes, at any rate."

"They're already eating us out of house and home!"

"They're our guests, Millie dear." She smiled at Ryan. "We can drive to Kohl's soon."

Ryan yawned. Millie walked him back to his room and tenderly put him into bed. Outside, cars drove by, bass drum thumping out their windows.

"How long have we been here?" asked Mark finally. Ryan hadn't thought he was awake.

"Haven't we always been here?"

"I don't know." Mark stared up at the ceiling. "I remember being somewhere else."

"Well, it couldn't have been better than here," Ryan said. Mark turned on his side and soon Ryan heard his breathing slow down into sleep. Ryan searched his memory, reaching into the places where there was only mist and fog. He knew there was *something* there. Sometimes he remembered a woman, his mother he supposed, and a room full of children. He'd read about other children's lives in books, and he thought the room might be a school.

He knew one thing, though. He was right. Life with Vincel and Millie was better than anything that came before, because when he saw the dimly recalled places of his past, Mark wasn't anywhere in them.

The traveler had won the gold rings at cards in a winemaking town, a place where the vineyard-keepers spent the winter caring for their casks as tenderly as a new mother for a baby. The badgering it took even to get a group of players together at the tavern one night was such that the traveler did not expect she would be welcome to return to the town. Especially because she'd taken so much of their money and then, at the last, the rings, from a weeping young man who'd intended to give them to his beloved on Christmas Day.

He should have been a better card player if he'd wanted to keep those rings, Millie thought.

From the house in the forest Millie traveled southwest, skirting the great mountains and following the river toward the sea. Her goal over these six summer months was to earn as much money as she could, and she knew that meant, in many of her stops, taking advantage of the relationships she'd made over her years of travel. The winemaking town wouldn't be the only place she wouldn't be welcome when she was done.

At a grand house in the foothills she was greeted warmly by a countess who loved her. (The count did not care for her, as he did not care for any woman, including his wife.) There she drew new portraits of the lady's children and a favorite serving girl and enchanted the chickens so that they stopped laying eggs. Even from inside the house she could hear the consternation of the cook, who clucked and paced like the hens she cared for. For a week she spent her days flirting with the countess and her children and her nights brewing a potion in her chamber. Finally she announced to the household that she had a solution that would return the chickens to their former productivity. All that she would require, she told the anxious cook, was payment of the first egg each of the chickens laid.

After the cook consulted with the lady of the house, it was agreed. The household assembled in the courtyard, all but the count, who was out at the hunt. Millie poured the potion into the chickens' feed from a small vial. The crowd, twenty people strong, murmured and covered their faces at its odor. The chickens, though, pranced straight over and devoured the feed, jostling one another to get at the trough.

"How long will it take?" the countess asked, her hand over her nose.

"No time at all," said Millie. And indeed the chickens were already bustling off toward their roosts, clucking anxiously. Soon there appeared underneath each of them a single egg, each larger than the last. And at the end of the henhouse, the bewildered rooster had laid a very small egg of pure gold.

An uproar! Shouting, hissing, dark looks at the traveler in the household's midst. The cook's husband stood at the rooster's nest, his face as red as the rooster's comb. It was only after Millie made a pronouncement about how a debt unpaid might leave *all* the women of a house unable to fill their nests that he stepped aside, grudgingly, and allowed Millie to take the egg in her hand. It was heavy, soft, and flat on one end.

"Take your egg," the countess said, the pain at her betrayal clear in her face. "Take all your eggs. But you must leave before my husband returns from the hunt, for he will not stay his hand when he learns a witch has been in our house."

A small treasure in her pocket; another home to which Millie could never return. Ah, no matter, for the world was large and full of places for her to go with her beloved. She boiled the eggs over a fire that night, and when she ate one for her supper, she thought of the enchanted egg the daughter had given her. The spell hadn't been necessary; she always intended to return. But she loved Vincel even more to taste her touch when she bit into the egg.

And so Millie's summer went, with tricks and traps played on those who had once thought her a friend. But she wasn't a friend, she was a sharp of the road, a wild thing, and it was better they knew. She had been a friend to no one in her life until Vincel, had felt tenderness but no obligation to any person. But now the love she felt for that young woman in her warm house, and the mother who bore her, was different from anything she'd felt before, and she knew she was ready for the transformation to come.

Millie left a trail of broken hearts across the valleys and plains that summer. But they were worth the breaking, for the one whole and true heart that awaited her come autumn.

The last morning of summer, Millie stopped her horse for a drink at a stream a dozen miles from Vincel's house. Puffy white seeds floated through the sunbeams like snow. The horse was a prize from a landowner for finding his lost son and heir—a son, ardent and brainless, whom Millie herself had lured into a cave and then drugged to sleep. No doubt the landowner, when the son regained the power of speech, was furious, but by then Millie was miles and miles away thanks to her fine reward. Maybe she should just cross the whole southwest off the map, she thought. Head east with her bride, or south over the mountains to the peninsula, there to eat clams by the sea.

"That's a fine horse."

A man stood on the other side of the brook. How had he approached without her observing him? Millie cursed herself for daydreaming and held the reins tighter.

The man noticed. "I have no designs on her, I assure you," he said. "I never learned to ride."

"You'd have trouble riding her even if you were a knight," Millie said. "She won't abide anyone but me on her back." This was a bald lie; the horse, fast and stupid, would let the devil himself mount her, if he had a carrot.

The man gestured toward the stream. "May I?" She nodded. He hopped across, one stone to the next, as lightly as a dancer, and on her side of the brook stooped to fill his canteen. His hair was silver and his clothes dapper but worn. Millie had long experience judging men on the road, and this one, spry though he was, posed little danger.

She mounted the horse and secured her pack. The man looked up, anxious. He said, "May I accompany you? I have not been in these parts for many years, and without the guidance of someone who knows these woods I will lose my way."

Millie considered. It was true the forest paths, winding and rife with thieves, were no place for a man of his age to wander aimlessly. She did not really want company, but supposed she could bear it for a few miles.

The man was grateful. Walking alongside Millie as the horse made its way down the road, he introduced himself as Bernd and of-fered her a cake. He'd lived quite a life, from his telling, and despite herself Millie came to enjoy the chatter about his tour as a soldier, his time as a student, his life as a doctor and dentist in a village in the mountains. Millie clicked her tongue and chuckled at the stories of his trade, full of gruesome tooth extractions.

"I spent some time on the road when I was your age," he said as they made their way through a wood of towering pines, the needles soft under their feet. "It's a hard life, but one with rewards."

"I've found those rewards," Millie replied. "I'm to be married soon."

"Congratulations, young traveler," Bernd said.

As they walked, Millie weighed the possibility of swindling Bernd. He'd been a doctor, and he carried a purse like hers, but she thought she'd likely leave him alone. His clothes and his manner didn't suggest real wealth, and she preferred to work against the rich, those who didn't deserve what they had and would barely miss what they lost. And anyway, she liked the old man. She saw in his past a little of her own wildness and saw in his contentment a little of her own future.

As they walked, she told him of her travels. Not the incriminating parts, but the places she'd been and the portraits she'd drawn.

"And you're to be married!" he said. "I remember the joy of discovering one who loves you." He chuckled. "I'm long past that, of course."

"You're not so old," said Millie. "You're traveling now."

"Only because I have nowhere to be," the man said. His village had been destroyed by an avalanche, God's hand rumbling down the mountain, he'd said, and wiping the earth clean so that no trace remained.

"Nevertheless, that takes spirit and strength."

He sighed. "I thank you. Spirit and strength can only get me so far. I need money. I'm traveling to the city of my birth, in hopes that I can find work there."

Late in the afternoon, they approached an inn deep in the pines, just a few miles from Millie's destination. Millie liked the old man but did not wish to get any closer to the house in the woods with him. She dismounted and said, "This is where I must part ways with you. I know this inn and trust the keeper."

"I think I recognize it, from my time in this country, decades ago," Bernd said.

She took a coin from her purse and handed it to him. "This will pay for your stay. Thank you for your company and your stories."

The man took the coin. "That's generous," he said. "I hope our paths cross again."

There was a fluttering and rustling in the trees. Bernd pointed and Millie looked. A large snowy owl had alighted on a branch just ten feet away. It was beautiful. Slowly the owl rotated its head until it met Millie's eye.

She gasped. Bernd grabbed her arm. Then she blinked, uncomprehending, for on the branch where the snowy owl had sat now perched Bernd, smiling merrily. She looked down at her arm where he had touched it. The owl screeched at her, pecked at her ear, and then leapt from her sleeve. It was gone in three flaps of its great wings.

Bernd crouched with unnatural balance on the thin bough, which bent under his weight. In his hand he held a purse, which Millie knew at once was hers. She touched her waist. A purse remained tied there, but it felt different. It was his. "You're an enchanter," she said.

He nodded. "As are you. But you're young, still, and did not recognize me in time."

Millie sought a trick that might recover her purse before it was too late. Nothing came to mind. "I trusted you. I was generous," she said.

"Ah, as generous as the lords and ladies whose coins fill this bag were to you, before you broke their trust." He tested the bough, leapt like a bird to one higher. "And what is that horse you ride but a sign of the trust someone once had in you?"

"I need that money," Millie said.

Bernd laughed. "As do I," he said. "You may keep my treasures, though, in return." And then he was away, springing from branch to branch, far faster than she could follow.

The road was empty. Next to her the horse nickered quietly. An owl, or maybe Bernd, hooted in the distance. She opened the purse at her waist. It was full of teeth.

The boys slept in the same bed, curled into each other like quotation marks. The room was at the back of the house and looked out on nothing but trees; the boys slept soundly, the drapes closed against the day. When an obscure sadness found Ryan in his sleep, he found comfort there, in Mark's arms, in Mark's face, in Mark's warm breath.

In the evenings the boys helped to clean, collected herbs from the yard, assisted Vincel with her sculptures. The rock tumbler rattled through the night, polishing eyes. They read books, old novels with cracked spines and library books the ladies brought back in the pickup truck. They even learned to help with dinner: how to prepare a roast or how to steam broccoli.

But mostly the boys sat on the couch and listened to the story. Sometimes Vincel spoke, and sometimes Millie; sometimes Ryan heard Vincel's voice though Millie's lips were moving, or heard Millie's voice out of a photograph on the mantel. None of this was frightening. He held Mark's hand and waited to hear what happened next. And when the dawn approached, he nestled next to Mark in the bed in the room at the back of the house. Sometimes they kissed each other to sleep; sometimes they fumbled with each other's bodies. Vincel washed their sheets with a fond smile.

On the first night of fall, no daughter sat in the window waiting for a visitor. No song rang out from the forest near the little house.

That night, instead of waiting eagerly for her beloved, Vincel dozed in a chair at her mother's bedside. Her mother slept much of the

time, but also ate, drank, wept, needed. The daughter helped her with
the bedpan and changed the hay in the mattress when things went
wrong. She fed her mother boiled vegetables and berries. And she did
all the work of the house, fetching the water and cutting the wood
and digging the carrots and cooking the meals and mending the broken door. The days were getting shorter, and Vincel never had time
or energy or enchantment enough for everything she had to do. The
hens were gone. The garden was overrun by moles. Only the cat was
happy, well-fed by the mice who multiplied in the walls.

That night, instead of singing cheerfully outside her beloved's
window, Millie sat with her back against a fallen tree, drinking a sto-
len bottle of wine and ruing her lost fortune. She'd dared to dream
of a different sort of life for herself, one filled with love, and she had
proven herself unworthy. She had made a promise she couldn't keep,
just another broken confidence in a long line that seemed now to define her life. She pulled another tooth from Bernd's purse, cursed it
as she had cursed all the rest, and then flung it into the darkness. It
blazed a bright trail like a shooting star and bounced off a branch. Far
off through the trees she saw another light, the flicker of a candle at
the house in the forest. The night was getting colder and she had nowhere to stay, no money to pay for a room. She pulled herself to her
feet, dropped the wine bottle, and led her big, stupid horse toward the
candlelight.

At first light Vincel woke with a start. The house was warm,
somehow, though she hadn't had the energy to build a fire. Her mother
slept quietly in the bed, but she herself had been covered by a blanket in her chair. She opened the shutters, which someone had closed,
and blinked in surprise. A large brown horse stared at her from the
yard.

In the house's central room the coals of a fire glowed in the hearth.
Before it, on the floor, slept Millie. She was dirty and her hair was

unkempt and she wore a brand-new suit of clothes. Vincel thought she'd never seen anyone so lovely in all her life.

After that morning, Millie stayed with Vincel and her mother in the house. She chopped wood and chased off the moles and found new chickens—she never said where. She rode the horse to market and struck bargains that Vincel found suspiciously weighted in their favor. She hauled Vincel's bed into the main room and there the two lovers delighted in their evenings. She sat for hours telling stories to the mother while Vincel walked in the forest gathering mushrooms and enjoying her solitude.

They found that the tricks they could work were far more effective together than they had ever been alone. With their own hands, gimmel rings sparkling, they could make drinks that soothed the mother's pain, soil that nurtured tastier beans, salves that eased their aching muscles. When the garden needed sun they could encourage the fog to dally somewhere else.

In the mother's final months, it was summer again. Vincel and Millie threw open the window and let her look out at the birds in the trees. Sometimes she sang to them, and once Vincel walked into the room to see a starling perched on the windowsill, its head tilted, its eyes locked on the mother's. The starling took one look at Vincel, trilled, and flew away.

They buried the mother in the forest on the first day of autumn. When they returned to the house, Vincel sat heavily at the table. She'd cried all the tears she had to cry. She said, "You may travel now, if you wish. You have no further obligation to me, and I do not want to keep you from the life you love."

Millie bent to kiss her, then took an egg from the basket hanging by the window. With a touch of the hand she boiled it, then rapped it once onto the windowsill. There it sat. "I am where I wish to be," Millie said.

They stayed together at the table for a while, Vincel's head on Millie's shoulder. Outside, the birds sang and the horse whinnied. Then there was a knock at the door. It was Bernd.

"Bernd!" said Mark as the boys got ready for bed. "What's he doing there?"

"I think he's Vincel's father," Ryan said.

"Oh! He said he'd been there before!"

"Right. And all we know about Vincel's dad is that he was gone before she was even born."

The boys often discussed the night's tale while they changed into the pajamas the ladies had left for them in the room's chest of drawers, pajamas so old and soft they must have been worn by generations of children before them.

"He can be birds! I bet he's the bird who visited her mom!"

"Yeah, that's what I think, too."

"Good night, boys," said Vincel from the doorway.

But before they settled into bed, they heard a crash outside. Voices laughed and shouted in the dark of the yard. Millie cried out from the living room: "Little monsters! I'll ruin them!" And Vincel, fearful: "No, Millie, no"—

Another crash. It was the statues, the boys realized. Someone was attacking the statues. Together they bolted out of their bedroom, through the living room, past the protesting women, and then they burst through the porch doors into the gloom. Near the side window they saw, amid the silent, unmoving figures, shadows moving with purpose. Someone hooted as another statue tipped over. A beer can clanked off the side of the house.

Ryan and Mark shouted and ran toward the shadows. The people scattered like ghosts. One ran past Ryan toward the porch, tripped over a toppled statue, and tumbled to the ground. Ryan turned around and advanced, yelling "Get out of here! Get out!" When the porch light came on, he saw a kid in a White Sox cap holding his knee. He looked up at Ryan in surprise and fright.

"Why are *you* here?" he asked, then scrambled to his feet and ran down the path.

Vincel clucked over the boys, helping them clean up the cuts on their bare feet from running around the yard. Even Millie seemed less grumpy than usual. She might have even looked a little proud. "Vincel?" asked Ryan.

"Yes, my dear?"

"Is Bernd your father?"

Vincel smiled. She said, "The story will continue, and you will be right here to hear it."

Standing in the doorway, Bernd resembled in no way the poor, polite traveler Millie had met by the creek. His clothes were very fine and his face bore a scornful smile. "Well, this is a charming house," he said.

Vincel stood stoutly before him. "And who is this who visits our home?"

He raised an eyebrow. "*Our* home?" He looked past Vincel to Millie, aghast at the table. "Such a prize you have won in my daughter, traveler."

"I knew it!" said Ryan.

Vincel did not gasp or cry out but looked at Bernd appraisingly. "Your daughter, you say. We'll see about that."

Millie stood. "Be careful, Vincel. I don't know if he's your father but I do know he is a sorcerer."

"As are you," Bernd said to Millie. "As is your bride. And where do you think it comes from? Your mother had no magic in her."

"What do you know of my mother?" Vincel asked evenly. "You were far away."

"I know she was as plain as milk. Now. I'd like to come in." And such was his power that Vincel stood aside. Bernd bent the requirements of hospitality so that both women were forced to cook and serve him dinner, though both were bone-tired from their toil. On the day that she had buried her mother, Vincel found herself wringing a chicken's neck so that Bernd could have meat in his soup. On the day she had dug a grave and let her bride cry on her shoulder, Millie found herself mending a hole in the sole of Bernd's shoe, grimacing and muttering all the while. Oh, how she wished to leap to her feet and stab him in his smirking face with the awl, but around himself he built a nest of spells that made it impossible to fight him. When her thoughts even neared such a notion, she found her head rang like bells.

When he had eaten and drunk his fill he wiped his mouth, rose, and walked toward the door. "I'll be back tomorrow, daughter," he said. "See that your stew has more flavor." And in a flurry of feathers he was gone into the night.

Vincel sank to the floor in agony, and Millie rushed to her side. Poor Vincel wept, for not only was she exhausted and mourning her mother, Bernd had laid in her mind all the loyalty and love a child ought to feel for a father—though he had earned none of that. And yet there it was, a daughter's fealty, as whole in her heart as if the man had raised and cared for her since her birth. She felt it as strongly as she felt her love for her mother or for Millie, and thus his cruelty opened a hole in her. "I'll kill him," exclaimed Millie, whose mind was clearer now that he was gone, but Vincel only tore at her hair and said "No, no, no," for she would die if something were to happen to him.

The next day was rainy and windy and the women worked hard to protect the crops, to keep the animals safe, to keep the house dry. All through the day Millie hoped that Bernd's promise would not be kept, but at dusk she saw a great black crow perch on the handle of the pitchfork, and then there Bernd was, leaning on the fork with a hat tilted jauntily on his head. His silver hair was newly cut and he smiled to see Vincel fluttering out of the house to greet him. Millie despaired at Vincel's abject love.

"The garden is a mess, daughter," he said. "I hope the house is clean for my arrival." And he walked through the door, leaving the women outside.

"Don't listen to him," Millie said. "He only wants to hurt you." But Vincel stood up straight, shook her head, and followed him into the house.

And for a time this was the way things were: All day Vincel would work, and Millie, working alongside her, would gently tell her that Bernd was wrong—that she had worth, that she was not a disappointment, that her love for him oughtn't excuse the way he spoke to her. Millie hated to call it love, this cruel charm, but when she tried to speak to Vincel frankly about what Bernd had done, Vincel became upset and pushed her away. And then at dusk Bernd arrived, and the women waited on him like servant-girls, Millie seething with hatred, Vincel desperate with need. He sat in their chair like a king, his feet on the table, hogging the fire and eating all that they brought him, the best of the garden and the surrounding woods.

And while he leaned back in his chair he told Vincel of how he had met her poor, uneducated mother in the woods, and how he had dazzled her with the easiest of tricks and the cheapest of luxuries, for she had never before tasted a lemon. And because she was simple, like her daughter, she had fallen in love with him, though he had never truly been that interested in her. He who had entertained the ladies of the court of the Habsburgs! He who had flown to Iberia and eaten the figs from the trees! What intrigue could a dull peasant girl hold for him? But she fed him and doted on him and who was he to turn down such treatment. Soon enough she had given herself to him completely, but then she became pregnant, and the idea of enduring the squalling of a brat? No, better to fly away, though she clung to him so.

He didn't sleep at the house. He showed no interest in their money, or their bodies, for which Millie was grateful. All he wanted was their solicitous attention, and to cause them pain, and then to depart after dinner, off doing whatever it was he did.

And while Bernd's daytime absence weakened the weave of his enchantment over Millie, she still found she could not truly plot against him—could not hide a knife, could not poison his food. To her despair the protection even guarded against silly offenses; she couldn't even spit in his beer, she learned when her mouth dried so unnaturally that she couldn't speak. And of course there was no fighting his enchantment with one of her own; she was nowhere near strong enough, not without Vincel's help.

But what Millie could do, late one night after he was gone and after Vincel had fallen asleep, was sit by the embers of the fire and then cut the tiniest notch in the leg of the chair. She did it so quickly her mind hardly knew what she had done—but she also had focused every last bit of energy and craft she could summon to sit in this spot, to let herself drift above the warp and weft of his spell, and to apply the knife ever so briefly to the soft wood of the chair leg. After it happened she ran roaring into the night. She couldn't think about what she'd done, but when the pain abated she knew without knowing that she had done something, at least.

The next night, she did it again. It hurt even more, but she could just about stand it.

For the tightening and slackening of Bernd's control over her had convinced her that it was a spell on which he had to concentrate. In fact, she was quite certain that for all his casual cruelty and off-hand cheer he was actually working very, very hard to maintain his hold over the women. She was also quite certain that he wasn't used to working this hard, that for most of his life he had flitted from mark to mark, woman to woman, gaining their trust and breaking it as easily as he had done Vincel's mother's (and, she knew, her own). But by committing to this daily trial, he had locked himself into a grueling battle, and Millie hoped he couldn't keep this level of concentration up forever.

Each day the women worked. Each evening Bernd ate the product of their toil and made Vincel dance like a marionette. Each night Vincel sank deeper into misery and self-hatred, and Millie sank the knife just a tiny bit deeper into the chair leg. This went on for a month, and Millie felt the women couldn't last much longer. They were gaunt from hunger and overwork; Vincel was so lost in duty and despair she barely spoke. And Millie's pain was constant, the offenses accumulating on her conscience, all her energy spent hiding what she'd done and gathering the courage to do it once more. They would need to act, and act soon.

"And the worst part is, they're haranguing these poor girls who are just trying to get into the clinic. As if they don't have it hard enough!"

"*That's* the sin," Vincel said.

Millie snorted. "That ridiculous word. But you're right, this time. The ancient judges would treat them harshly."

Vincel gave a contented sigh. "Look at that beautiful sunset ahead," she said.

Even Millie couldn't be angry about that. "I see it," she said.

Mark and Ryan were sitting in the jump seats in the back of the pickup, looking through the rear window at the trees disappearing behind them, their newly orange leaves. In the pickup bed rested three long logs—limbless trees, really. Millie wanted to try making totems.

From this odd angle everything was receding away from them: that store, those people waiting at the bus stop, the traffic light dangling over the intersection.

"Oh my!" Vincel cried, and at that moment, a car broadsided them from the left, smashing into the bed of the truck. With a screech and a shriek the truck spun, bouncing to a stop after a half-turn, the boys now pointed directly at that glorious sunset. As the light flooded the back of the cab, Ryan, too, felt flooded, as suddenly he remembered: remembered his home, remembered his school, remembered his family, so far away and forgotten so long. He saw from the look on Mark's face that at the moment of impact he, too, had felt all this sweeping back.

"Boys!" Vincel called. "Are you hurt?" A passing police car turned on its lights and pulled up behind them. The officer helped Vincel and Millie from their seats and sat them on a bench on the corner. The other car was a mess, its driver bleeding from the scalp and shouting angrily at the cop.

Mark sidled up to Ryan as they stood on the curb. "Did you feel that?" he said.

"I still feel it," Ryan said.

A little dazed, they watched the ladies, who were talking to the officer. The policeman knelt down between them, listening and taking notes. Mark and Ryan came over, stood on the curb, alive to the fear in the women's eyes as they looked to the officer, to the boys, and back.

The policeman turned to face the boys. "Do these ladies belong to you?" he asked. Ryan hesitated for a moment. He thought about Vincel and Millie, and how much he trusted them, their gentle care and the beautiful things they made together. He thought about how much he loved Mark, and how much Mark, he knew, loved him, and how fragile that was, and how it could fall apart if it wasn't protected. He recalled what Vincel had said: "You will be safe for as long as you wish to stay." And Ryan thought about the story, and the peril the women faced, and how close they were to the end.

Mark caught his eye, smiled, placed a kind hand on his arm. Ryan turned to the policeman. "Yes," he said. "We all belong to each other."

The night was crisp and Bernd insisted upon a fire. "I am old and my bones creak, and you are too lazy to build a fire to keep me warm?" he said, and Vincel scurried to collect wood. Millie, for her part, kept her gaze on the meal she was cooking; she knew that if she met eyes with her despised enemy for even a moment, he would see what she had done.

The firewood was damp and didn't want to ignite. Vincel worked in a frenzy, withering under Bernd's criticism and complaints. Finally the flame caught and Vincel stepped away from the hearth. "Vincel, come here, please," Millie said. "I need your help with this bread."

"It's no wonder your loaves are so tough, with two sets of hands working on them," Bernd grumped, but Millie could tell his heart wasn't in it. He was focused on the warmth of the fire as he leaned back, picking at his fingernails.

Vincel, eyes downcast, came to Millie at the counter. Millie laid her hand on her beloved's so that their two rings gently *clink*ed against each other. She thought of the one spot on one particular log where a tiny bubble of water was trapped under a knot, and together with Vincel she brought the fire just a bit closer and set that bubble to a boil—

CRACK! An ember flew from the fire and landed on Bernd's fine shirt and he scrambled to brush it off and leaned farther back and—

SNAP! The leg of the chair collapsed and Bernd fell backward and cracked his head on the floor.

And in that moment, it was as if sunbeams burst through the roof of the cottage, burning through the fog, casting the light of truth upon all within. Vincel saw with instant clarity that she owed Bernd nothing, that he had no true power over her—that what she'd seen as her duty was obligation and illusion, not love. She grasped Millie's hand so hard that Millie had fingernail marks on her skin a day later. Together they broke every spell that Bernd had placed upon them and the house. And while Bernd lay on the floor muttering curses, the two women embraced.

"Now," Millie said, turning to Bernd. "Now you shall serve *us*."

But after a few hours of Bernd bowing and apologizing and sweeping the house, they found themselves bored with him. He had nothing to offer them, not even his abject humiliation. They opened the door and banished him into the night. Here he exits their story, never to return.

The two women lived together in peace in the little house for the rest of their lives. They tended their garden, they cared for their chickens, they carved small wooden figures which they sold at the market to townspeople who wanted just a little bit of good luck. They traveled to the mountains, so Vincel could feel the cold breath of a glacier on her cheek. They traveled to the sea, so Vincel could sit on a ship's stern and watch the land disappear behind them. And when, after forty years together, Millie began to lose herself, Vincel cared for her in the house's bedroom. Millie lay quietly in the bed as Vincel's mother had before, and Vincel fed her and washed her and held her hand. And at the very end, in that house that was full to the rafters with love, Vincel sang,

I will remember
The touch of your hand,
Every sunrise,
This gold gimmel band.

And Millie, eyes closed, joined her:

> *And if you remember the love that we share*
> *Then find me again as the bird finds its nest.*
> *For you are my home and my darling so rare*
> *This gimmel ring shared with the one I love best.*

The house itself was soon covered in vines and filled with animals. And its wood rotted and its stone collapsed and now, deep in the forest, you could walk across it and never know it was there. But if you stopped at the right spot and combed through the moss and the stones and the wild beanstalks, you might find two golden bands, joined together at a hinge.

"What?" said Ryan.

"You're right here in front of us," Mark said. "You didn't die in a house in the woods a million years ago!"

"They'll never understand," said Millie, clearing the mugs of cider from the coffee table. Outside it was once again cold winter. The boys sat on the couch as always, dressed now in the clothes Vincel had bought for them.

"Oh, my ducks." Vincel rose from her chair and hunted through the papers stacked up on the desk in the corner. "That Vincel and that Millie died in that house—well, not a million years ago, but a long time ago. Then another Vincel and another Millie were born and found each other. And another, and another, and now there's us in this house in Hampton Heights. We've spent our lives here in Milwaukee, teaching and marching and telling our stories to anyone who will listen."

Millie returned from the kitchen. "Not that anyone really listens," she said.

Vincel waved her off. "Oh, now you have been wonderful company this past year. You're polite and kind boys, and I hope that you remain close long after you've forgotten all about us."

"Forget about you?" asked Ryan.

"Ah, there it is," said Vincel, and she pulled out a clipboard and envelope. She seemed just a tiny bit sad, though Ryan couldn't imagine why.

"Put us down for a year's subscription, I suppose," Millie said, and Mark eagerly wrote the name she gave on his clipboard. When Ryan asked how she wanted to pay, she snapped, "You can bill us."

"Well, thank you for the cider and the cookies," Mark said.

"Yeah, thank you. They were really good." Ryan got up and looked around for his coat. Oh, there it was, hanging by the door. Boy, he really needed to get his mom to buy him a new one. This one was getting really small. Thank god he was finally growing a little!

It was torturously cold outside after their bodies had gotten used to the warmth of the old ladies' house. "Another sale!" Mark exclaimed as they walked down the path.

"These statues are pretty cool, honestly," said Ryan. "I think those old ladies made them all."

"They're really creative," agreed Mark.

Ryan elbowed Mark. Outside the fence, the two neighborhood kids waited. They looked like people who were very impressed but were trying not to show it. "You went *in?*" the big one asked.

"It was no big deal," said Mark.

The little one shook his head. "When you went in there, I thought, *Damn.* I was sorry I talked it up, because I thought you were dead."

Ryan laughed. "They're not witches or whatever. They're nice old ladies. They bought a subscription."

"All right," the little one said. He held out a hand and Mark shook it. "Good luck with your magazines or whatever. Don't be comin' to my house trying to sell that." The kids ambled around the corner and were gone.

"Oh jeez," Ryan said, looking at his watch. "It's almost nine."

"Well, I guess we sold two subscriptions. I wonder if everyone else did better."

Ryan was surprised to find that all his old awkwardness around Mark was gone. He slapped him on the back and said, "No one had a better time than we did, though."

Mark laughed. "Say no more," he said in his best British accent.

They headed back up the block, shoving each other and laughing. They both knew that something extraordinary had happened to them, but they didn't have the words for what it was. In the weeks after they got home, their parents made quizzical comments about how they were growing so fast they couldn't even keep up, and how they'd had to buy all new clothes. Ryan, as tall as everyone else now, actually did okay in gym class.

And even after everything else that happened that night, Ryan remembered to exchange phone numbers with Mark. They remained friends for years, and though they only sort of remembered their time inside the women's house, they did recall bits and pieces of the story they'd heard, and sometimes even tried to puzzle out its lost details with each other. Once they drove together to Hampton Heights; the neighborhood was mostly unchanged, only a little more bedraggled, but they couldn't find the women's house. There were no statues. There was nothing on the corner but an empty, wooded lot.

Even after distance separated them, they thought of each other fondly. They both married; Mark and his wife had a daughter, as did Ryan and his husband. Years later, as the witches had promised, those daughters would finally meet.

AL AND NISHU

Alessandro Cotrone's mom called him Business Al. "A little hustler," she said, with bewilderment but also affection.

In fifth grade, when they'd moved from his grandparents' place into the town house, he'd spent a whole morning putting his markers, baseball cards, and Trapper Keepers into the drawers of his new room's desk. His own room! A desk built into the wall! On each side of the desk were three wooden drawers; all told, there was space for nearly everything he owned. It was an enormous improvement over sharing a room with his mom and doing his schoolwork at the dining room table while his grandfather yelled at the television.

Several of the drawers contained old paper clips or thumbtacks or, in one case, a dead moth. Most of them were sticky and required big tugs to haul them open, and the drawers gave great groans as they scraped against the rails inside. So when Al, sitting on the floor in a pile of construction paper, got to the bottom left-hand drawer, he gave it a mighty pull, but it slid as smoothly as Cecil Cooper into second. In fact, the drawer flew all the way out of the cabinet. Al fell backward and whacked his head on his bedframe.

As he tried to lift the drawer back in, he saw that there was an empty space between the rails and the floor. He might not have noticed the space, except that a beautiful woman looked up at him from under there. She wasn't wearing any clothes. She was on the cover of a *Playboy* magazine.

It was the middle of the afternoon. His mom had to work after church, and he was alone in the house. The woman on the cover invited him closer. She had red hair. Her arms were crossed in such a way that Al could almost see her nipples. Inside the magazine, he understood instantly, she would uncross her arms. He didn't think, even for a second, about not pulling the magazine out and opening it.

There were a lot of long articles. There were cartoons with drawings of butts and boobs in them. But for now he didn't care about that. He flipped through the pages until he found the woman from the cover, her red hair swirling around her face, her breasts—oh!—her breasts revealed.

Yes, it was a sin, he knew, to stare at this woman, at all the women in the magazine, at the secret places they showed, secrets he never thought he'd get a chance to see. His priest would be mad. His mom would be furious. But that didn't stop him from staring at the photographs so long that he basically memorized them. Their skin was so smooth, and their smiles were so bright. They looked positively delighted to be caught, underpants halfway down, leaning against bales of hay.

The next day the word was whispered from fifth grader to fifth grader. At the bike racks when the school day was done, a dozen boys gathered around Al. The boys joked nervously with one another as he pulled the *Playboy* from his backpack, showing just the top half of the woman on the cover. (Her name was Susan, and her turn-ons included mustaches, massages, and a great sense of humor.) Mike Renner was the first to step forward, hand Al four quarters, and be granted one minute with the magazine. Al borrowed Mike's digital watch, which also transformed into a robot, to keep the time.

The group fell reverently silent while Mike hunched over the magazine. "Oh, man," he said at one point, but mostly he just paged through, stopping here and there to admire a particular photo. When Al said, "Time," he nodded, closed his eyes, folded the centerfold back into the magazine, and handed it back. "That was awesome," he said.

Al made nine dollars that day, and many classmates were desperately upset they'd spent their money on lunch. They wouldn't make the same mistake twice. Al made twenty-one dollars on Tuesday. By the afternoon, girls were asking to see the magazine as well. Noelle Meaux talked to him for the first time in recorded history when she paid him a dollar during the break between math and social studies and stood with her hands in his locker, holding the magazine, staring at Susan's centerfold with what Al thought seemed like professional appreciation. One perfect beauty admiring another. He was a businessman, but he gave her an extra ten seconds for free. She closed the magazine carefully, said, "Thanks, Al," and walked away.

One girl who didn't ask for a look was his friend Amy Friedman, the one person who'd really been nice to him in his first few weeks at this new school. He asked her if she wanted to see, told her she could do it for half price. "No thank you," she'd said. She didn't act offended or judgmental; she simply declined, as if he'd offered her a flavor of soda she didn't like. This was always, he would find, how she responded to his schemes, even the ones that didn't involve dirty magazines. She was his friend but she wasn't a hustler. This was back when she was talking to him still.

By the end of the day, seventh graders had started seeking him out and asking about the magazine. Plus, Susan was getting a little worse for wear. Cullen Mentink had tried to tear a page out. After the bell Al announced that this was the *Playboy*'s final day at school, and if anyone wanted a look at it, this was their last chance. He made more than thirty dollars.

It turned out this was the right move because the next morning they searched his locker. He could tell from Erica Rymer's expectant look, and her disappointment when Ms. Kohlmeier found nothing, that it had been her who'd ratted him out.

In the principal's office, Dr. Lawrence sat back in his chair, legs crossed. He had a ring of hair around his bald head and half-glasses he liked to peer over the top of. He looked down at Al over those glasses and said, "Why would someone make up a story like that?"

Al said he didn't know. Maybe because he was new?

Dr. Lawrence's eyes narrowed. He could tell the man didn't believe him, but he was almost certain that didn't matter. The *Playboy* was back under its drawer; the money was in his bedside table. He'd read enough Three Investigators books to know you couldn't nail anyone without a confession or hard evidence, and there was no way he was confessing.

He didn't get detention. Erica Rymer wasn't disciplined, either, for her story, which Al felt was outrageous. Of course they believed her over him. Okay, technically she was telling the truth, but nevertheless.

The principal did send a note to his mom, though. She read it after a long day at the nursing home. "Look, if you did this," she finally said, "you'll need to confess at church. I don't want to hear about it." It wasn't a coincidence, he figured, that she took him to the bank a few days later to open a savings account. When she saw how much he deposited, she laughed. "I suppose those kids can afford it," she said as she got in the car. The *Playboy* remained safe in his room. Who had his deception harmed? No one. A couple of fifth graders got a thrill. He got the money he needed. The women in the magazine got admired. Everyone won.

When Al learned you could get a paper route once you turned twelve, he signed up, even though the route was blocks away from his house, even though when his mom insisted on meeting the manager, Kevin had spent the whole conversation checking her out. The paper route made him a little cash—not enough for how much work it was, so early in the morning. But it also created other opportunities for Business Al. In the fall he saw which of the big houses on Lydell raked their yards and which didn't; the ones with leaves all over their lawns received flyers in their mailboxes advertising Al's Leaf Service. Al's Snow Service took over in the winter for the houses where no one got out early to shovel. He'd already picked out which of his customers had nice enough cars that they'd surely want to hire Al's Detailing in the spring.

What he wanted was money. With money, he could buy ice cream sandwiches in the cafeteria. With money, he could purchase baseball cards and movie tickets; with money he could, someday, afford a pair of Reeboks instead of the cheap shoes his mom bought him at Kohl's.

His mom wasn't a hustler. She was too tired, Al thought, from taking care of old people all day. But it was still better than before, when his mom couldn't find work and they lived with his grandparents in the house on 83rd Street. He had his own room. They both had jobs. And he had a bank account with $110 in it.

"Okay," Al said to Nishu as they walked away from the van. "I think we should split up."

"Aren't we supposed to stick together?" Nishu asked. He was wearing his backpack, which he had refused to leave in the van.

"He didn't actually say that."

Al could tell by the look on Nishu's face that he was a chicken. "I don't know," he said.

"Look, you want the twenty bucks, right?" Kevin had not specified whether the winning duo would split the twenty bucks or be awarded twenty bucks individually, but he kept that to himself.

"Yeah!" Nishu said fervently.

"If we split up we can hit twice as many houses. That's twice as many subscriptions we'll sell."

Nishu considered it as they crossed Hampton and headed north. "Maybe after we do a couple of houses together," he said finally. "I want to see how it goes."

Al decided to cut his losses for now and pressure him later. "Fine," he said. The first house on the list was right here, just up 53rd Street. They walked together up to the front door and Al rang the doorbell. After a long, long time—they were about to turn and go—they heard a shuffling on the other side of the door. With a creak the door opened, revealing an old man in pajama pants and a stained T-shirt. He looked down at the boys and said, "Yes?"

"We're selling subscriptions to the *Milwaukee Sentinel*," Al said crisply. "It's ten dollars for three months, or twenty-five for a year. If you subscribe for a year, you get a plate. We can take cash or you can pay later." That was everything on his checklist, he thought. "Would you like to subscribe?"

The man stared at them, then stuck his finger in his ear and wiggled it around. Finally he said, "What did you say you're selling?"

Oh, man. Al, annoyed, took a deep breath, but Nishu said, "The newspaper," and the man brightened.

"Oh, the newspaper!" he said. "Yes, I'll buy a newspaper from you boys."

"Great!" Al said. He had to ask three times to get the man's name, but eventually wrote it down on the clipboard: ERNEST FISCHER. Nishu asked Mr. Fischer if he'd like to pay now or later, and he said he'd pay now.

"How much do I owe?"

"Well, it's ten dollars for three months, or twenty-five for—"

"Ten dollars!" Mr. Fischer chuckled. "Oh, I see. Boys, I don't have that kind of money for a newspaper."

"No, it's for three months."

"I'm giving you ten dollars and you're bringing me a newspaper in three months?"

Al rubbed his eyes in dismay. They had already spent a hundred years on this guy's porch. Had he never heard of the concept of *subscribing* to a *newspaper*?! Nishu was clearly more patient than Al. He said, "Sir, you get the newspaper every day for three months."

"Oh," he said, waving his hand. "I don't need that many newspapers. I'll just take one. How much for just one?"

"We didn't bring the newspapers *with* us," Al said.

"You didn't bring the newspapers?" he asked, appalled. "You come here trying to take my money, and you don't have any newspapers?" And then he shut the door and, for good measure, turned off his porch light.

"Oh my God!!" Al exploded in the dark. "What the hell!"

"I can't believe that."

"He said yes!"

"It's not fair," Nishu agreed, taking the clipboard. He started erasing Mr. Fischer's name.

Al kicked at a little blue weed in the walkway in frustration. And then he had an idea. It appeared in his mind fully formed, as if someone had placed it there. "Wait a sec," he said. "Don't erase that."

Nishu stopped at the sidewalk junction. "What do you mean?"

Al plucked the clipboard from Nishu's hands. "Leave him on."

"But he said he doesn't want a subscription."

"He also said he *did* want a subscription."

When Al was going door to door, dropping off flyers, negotiating rates for raking or shoveling or whatever, he wasn't shy, even though generally he didn't like talking to people he didn't know. But Business Al didn't care. Business Al found the angle. Al hardly ever wore a tie, not even to church, but in his mind Business Al wore a tie everywhere.

He could almost feel that invisible tie now, cinched up around his neck, and it fed his outrage at this stupid old man who wasted their time, at this contest that made him dependent on stupid old men, at how he always needed money, always always. How even when he'd bought himself Reeboks, the other kids at his school had nicer Reeboks, or suddenly didn't like Reeboks anymore, had moved on to other shoes. How Aaron Sheahan got a Mongoose but always complained about how that bike sucked, he wanted a Supergoose, and then his dad bought him a Supergoose. Al's dad, safe in his apartment downtown with his new wife, would never buy him a Supergoose. Al rode the same old shitty Huffy he'd always ridden. It was so patently unfair, how other kids' parents just threw money at them, and his mom couldn't.

The idea grabbed him by the throat and he couldn't shake it off. It was too good an idea.

"Anyway, he doesn't know what he wants," Al continued.

"But he didn't pay!"

"I believe," Al said, deliberately checking a box on the clipboard, "that Ernest Fischer wants the *Milwaukee Sentinel* to bill him later."

Nishu looked back up at Mr. Fischer's house, now entirely dark. "I don't know," he said, his essential chickenhood once again on display.

Al started crossing the street toward the next house on the list. "Look, leave him on for now and let's hit some more houses. If we sell enough subscriptions, I'll erase him."

Nishu looked relieved to be presented with such a logical conclusion. "Okay, that makes sense."

Here was a way for him to win this contest, and no one would be harmed. A few people in Hampton Heights would get the newspaper. Eventually, they'd cancel, and the *Milwaukee Sentinel* would eat their subscription fees. The *Sentinel* could afford it. He delivered to forty-six houses every morning, each of them paying nearly five bucks a month for the paper, and each month in turn the paper paid him, like, thirty dollars. You didn't have to be a mathematician to understand how they were cleaning up on the deal.

"Should we split up?" Al asked. "That's how we'll really get the most."

"No, thank you." Nishu shook his head. In that moment he acted unnervingly like Amy Friedman. "I feel safer together."

Fine. Al didn't know what Nishu was afraid of. Monsters? But fine.

At the next house, the woman who answered the door turned them down flat. Didn't ask questions, didn't deliberate, just sent them on their way. "I respect that," Al said on the sidewalk. "She didn't waste our time."

At the next house, the man who answered the door seemed flat-out crazy. "Get away!" he shouted. "I see the mark of the vine around your neck! Leave me alone!" Al and Nishu left him alone. On the sidewalk, Al said, "We can stay together for a few more."

At the next house, a kid answered the door. He was little, maybe fourth grade. "Are your parents home?" Al asked.

"My mom's at the store," the boy said.

"You shouldn't answer the door when you're home alone," Nishu admonished.

"I'm not alone," the kid said happily. "George is here with me."

"Ah," said Al. He was getting a little impatient. His collar was itching and his hands were freezing holding the clipboard. "Who's George?"

"He's my friend."

Uncle, babysitter, whatever. It was time to move things along. "Does George like reading the newspaper?"

"Yes," said the boy. "He likes to know everything that's going on."

On the clipboard Al wrote GEORGE and 4847 N. 53RD ST. Nishu

looked scandalized, but Al ignored him. "I'll just put George down for three months, and we'll bill him later," he said. "Last question though—does George have a last name?"

The boy's face clouded and he looked at Al as if understanding, suddenly, that Al didn't know anything. "No," he said, and closed the door. Al finished the name: GEORGE NO.

"You can't do that!" Nishu hissed as they walked back to the sidewalk.

"Nothing's gonna happen," Al said.

"What about when they get the bill?"

"They'll pay it like all the other bills."

"They'll pay a bill for 'George No'?"

"Well, maybe not," he admitted. "But they'll get a good laugh out of it. 'Our kid ordered the newspaper for his imaginary friend!'"

"We'll get in trouble!"

Al stopped walking and laid a fatherly hand on Nishu's shoulder. "They are never, ever gonna know it was us."

Nishu considered this. "They won't?"

"We're never coming back here."

"Right. I guess."

Al told Nishu about last summer, when his mom totally freaked out because the water bill was a hundred bucks more than it was supposed to be. A man came from the water place and told them the toilet had a leak and was running water constantly. He fixed the leak and told her that the water company would cancel the charge, no problem.

Over the next week, Al got used to the sound of his mom arguing with the water people on the telephone. It was the daily accompaniment to his breakfast TV-watching, her exasperated phone calls. No one at the water company knew what the guy had been talking about. They didn't just cancel charges, ma'am. Or there was a department that handled adjustments, but they were only available in the afternoons. Or actually, the records didn't show that anyone from the water company had come to her house at all. "No, I don't remember his name," his mom said, despairing.

But then! One day they got an envelope in the mail from the water people with a check in it for *two* hundred dollars. So she tried calling the water company *again*, to tell them they sent her too much money. Al listened as she was transferred twice, explained the situation once again, and then hung up, shaking her head. The woman on the other end of the line had said, "Honey, no one here has any idea what you're talking about. Cash the check."

Al could tell, from the very fact that they hired someone like Kevin to manage kids like him, that the *Milwaukee Sentinel* was even more disorganized than the water company. Any connection between this canvassing expedition in a random Milwaukee neighborhood and the person in a building downtown who might someday try to bill George No twenty-five dollars was so tenuous as to be irrelevant. No harm would come to Al or Nishu, or this kid, or his parents. All that would happen was that Mr. Fischer and George would get the newspaper for a few weeks, and Al and Nishu would win twenty bucks.

This was why he was a hustler. Not because he got jobs. Because he had a knack for taking a problem and finding the angle. When you come to school with bologna in your lunchbox every day, you need to be able to convince people to trade with you. Nishu could learn a little something from him.

"We got to take charge," Al said now. "Guys like us, we're never going to just get handed the victory. But if we take charge, we can win, I know it."

"You're an optimist," Nishu said.

"Sure, I guess you could say that."

"You look at a situation and you say it's a good situation, even if it's bad." Nishu considered this. "It's a kind of lying, but it's hopeful."

Al laughed. "It's not lying! I'm just the only one willing to figure out how to make the bad situation good."

"You're very creative," Nishu said diplomatically.

"Thank you."

Indeed, the man who answered the door at the next house listened politely to their sales pitch, agreed that it was a shame he'd let his subscription lapse, mentioned several *Sentinel* columnists whose work he enjoyed, said he'd been meaning to renew and wasn't it lucky the boys had stopped by. He, too, wished to be billed later. HORACE JOHNSON went on the third line of the clipboard. Al couldn't help but feel he was being rewarded for his initiative.

His dad believed in luck. When things were going good, his dad loved to talk about how luck was on his side. His mom believed in God, of course—God and the priests at St. Monica's. She believed that one little slip was all it took to set a life careening down the wrong path. Al thought there probably was a God, or *someone* out there, but whatever he was he didn't care two farts about how Al spent his time.

So no one was watching you, but no one was looking out for you, either. And he wasn't about to trust his future to luck. If you were a short kid without money, luck was not naturally on your side. He bet the same was true for Nishu. Maybe Nishu was totally popular at his school, despite being a little nerdy, a little chicken, and from India besides. More likely his daily life was a version of Al's. So he needed to learn Al's lesson: You made your own luck. You made it by paying attention to the systems and finding every loophole. You made it by always, always staying hungry.

They fell into an easy conversation as they made their way up 53rd, crossing the street back and forth, following the list on the clipboard. (Now that they were making sales, it was no longer necessary to split up, and anyways, he liked Nishu's company.) Like Al, Nishu was in sixth grade. They went to different schools, although they would eventually go to the same high school if Al didn't move again. Nishu was born in America, it turned out; it was his parents who were born in India. He told a funny story about explaining baseball to his parents, who loved some sport called cricket and couldn't understand the American game. The two of them reminisced about August, when they'd both spent every night stuck to their radios, waiting for Paul Molitor to extend his hitting streak. "Thirty-nine games!" Nishu said. "That was the first time my dad listened to the Brewers with me. He said he respected someone working hard every day." He shrugged. "He is so boring."

Nishu had questions about being Catholic. He'd gone to church once with a friend after a sleepover, much to his parents' indignation. He wanted to know more about confession. Al thought he seemed like a kid who worried about his own sins, few though they might be.

"You're really in a little booth?"

"Yeah, like a phone booth. The priest's on the other side of, like, a grate."

"And you really confess *everything*?"

Al knew what he was talking about, and said, "No way. Probably some people do, but I just tell the priests what they want to hear and get out of there. They don't need to know all my business." In the end, for example, he had never told them about Susan who loved massages.

"But if you did something really bad, you could confess it, and you would get forgiven?"

"Poof," said Al. "It just goes away."

Deep under a culvert pipe on Fairmount an ancient creature stirred. It had traveled long ago from the darkest corner of Europe, across the thundering Arctic ice, somehow ending up in flat, terrible Wisconsin, where it had made itself a home. It was rugged and gnarled, as closely related to a tree as it was to a person. Its many fingers wound through the earth, poked through the frozen ground into the air, and felt the breeze in a hundred places. Its ears could hear a whispered conversation in Oconomowoc, if the conversation was about ill doings. Its nose could smell treachery a mile away. Its spirit had made its way through the earth and water of Hampton Heights, and now it lived everywhere.

The creature had slept for some time but tonight was different. Tonight it was awake to the minds and souls around it. Near, very near, it sensed ambition, worn like a mantle around a boy's shoulders. The boy might as well have been singing, his hunger was so evident. What the creature could do with such zeal! The creature smacked its lips. It had already been so easy to prod him in the right direction.

It unfurled its legs, the joints cracking like a river thawing in spring. It pushed its face deeper into the mud and muttered old words into the earth. Those words traveled through the ground in every direction, infiltrated the pipes and ducts and wiring of Hampton Heights. In every house, the words wafted from heating registers or trickled from sinks, waiting to be released.

Fortune was coming for Al Cotrone.

The man in the Milwaukee Tool shirt looked bewildered as he wrote his name and address on the clipboard. Maybe this was because he'd already said, "No thank you, I don't want a subscription." But his hands moved of their own accord, and he pulled his wallet from his back pocket. "I don't have the money for it right now," he said plaintively, counting out twenty-five dollars and handing it to Nishu. "Please give that back," he said, and closed the door.

"Al?" said Nishu. Through the square windows at the top of the wooden front door they could see the man's anguished face, staring at them. "What do I do with these?" He held the bills in the air with some distaste.

"I don't know," said Al. "I don't know what to do." It had gone really well, at first. Pretty soon they didn't even need to do fake subscriptions because everyone just started saying yes. They probably had a hundred bucks in the envelope. But things had started getting really weird. One woman had insisted upon buying a subscription not only for herself but for her next-door neighbor. Another appeared to be trying to speak through their whole encounter, but all that came out of his mouth was the sound of the wind. He marked himself down for a three-month subscription. And then this guy, who had clearly not wanted to subscribe but had nonetheless handed them money and who now sounded like he was weeping on the other side of the door.

Nishu opened the mail slot to give the money back, only to reveal the man's wide eyes. "AAAAAAAHH!!" the man screamed, and Nishu stumbled backward. Al caught him before he could fall off the porch. They ran down the sidewalk and out the man's front gate and were two houses away before they stopped, hands on knees.

"Can we quit?" Nishu asked miserably. "We should quit. Don't we have enough?"

Al didn't understand how he could be so lucky and feel so guilty. What he was doing to these people seemed like a kind of torture, a torture that turned everything to his favor. Was this what it was like to be rich, to be powerful? No matter what people wanted, they find themselves pushing you farther and farther up the mountain? "This has got to be enough to win," Al said, looking at the clipboard, the order form full of names and addresses. "Let's go back."

A voice from the darkness made them both jump. "Are you the boys selling the newspapers?" An old man approached from a nearby yard. Bundled up against the cold, he walked slowly with a cane but seemed determined to reach them. "How much is a subscription?"

"Mister—"

"*How much?*" he demanded.

"It's twenty-five dollars for a year!" Nishu said.

"I want more than a year!"

The man stomped his feet in frustration, like a toddler having a tantrum. He started to say more but was interrupted by a woman jogging across the street in their direction. "I found you!" she called. She wore a housecoat and one slipper and shivered in the cold. "I thought I wouldn't be able to find you," she said, and burst into tears.

"Back off!" the man said.

Al held up his hands. "You can both, uh—" But the woman reached them before the old man could. She pressed close to the boys, waving a hand that still clutched, Al saw, a television's remote control.

"I'm Jackie Kern," she said breathlessly. "I live at 5119 Stark Street." Behind her the old man had finally made it to her and was muttering "Excuse me, excuse me," and without looking back at him she howled "GET AWAY!" in a deep and wounded voice. She dug in her housecoat pockets. "I know I have money somewhere," she said, "hold on . . ." As she patted herself Al saw the old man grip the cane with two hands and then swing it, connecting with the side of the woman's head. It made a sound like a perfect Paul Molitor double and she fell to her knees with a cry.

"Wait!" called Al, too late. It had already happened. But she looked up at him, eyes wide, blood drizzling on her housecoat, and moaned, "I'm sorry, can you bill me?"

The old man roared in anguish and rage. He took another step toward the boys, arms wide. He was about to grab Al, engulf him, when Nishu pulled on Al's arm, yelling "Come on come on come on!" And they were out, Nishu pounding down the sidewalk, Al right behind.

"*Come back here!*" the man shrieked, waving his cane. It wasn't hard to outpace him, but when Al looked back he could see that the woman had regained her feet and was chasing them. She was devilishly fast. Her other slipper must have flown off because Al could hear her bare feet slapping on the sidewalk.

There were other sounds. The neighborhood was waking up. Porch lights flipped on and storm doors opened. On front stoops, people pointed and took surprised, jerking steps. Al slipped a little on a patch of snow, almost lost his footing, kept going. He'd never been a fast kid. Nishu was well in front of him now.

But then Nishu froze at the corner. A couple was running at them down Fairmount. The man held a toddler, who screamed and squirmed in his arms. Her cries echoed across the block. "That's them!" the wife growled.

"No, no, no no no," Nishu said as Al caught up. Al's side hurt and his breaths were getting faster and faster, out of his control. This was all happening because of him, because of what he'd done. Why had he had this idea? Why had he given in to ambition?

Together they crossed to the kitty-corner, where a steel culvert emerged from the strip of lawn between the sidewalk and the street. He had an idea that maybe they could hide there, but all the customers could see them. They shambled toward the corner, demanding satisfaction.

That was when the creature stepped out of the culvert's mouth.

"Ugh!" Nishu said, jumping back.

The creature spread its four arms and said, "Though my—*oof!*" For Al, panicking, had kicked it as hard as he could. It bent the creature over sightly, but it totally wrecked Al's foot. It was like he'd kicked a tree. He hopped on one leg, swearing. The customers got closer.

The creature straightened officiously. It had only one eye, huge and red. "Though my appearance may be unusual," it said, as if nothing had happened, "I am the one who can solve your problem."

The shouting customers were steps away. "Unusual" was one way to put it, Al thought, but—"Yes! Solve it!"

The creature reached up with a gnarled hand and plucked its eye from its skull. Al, who couldn't even watch his mom put her contact lenses in, winced in revulsion, but the creature held the eye up in the air, where it blinked on its own. It was unusually large, crusty, and bloodshot. The customers halted, suddenly silent except for the toddler, who kept crying. The barefoot woman touched her head in wonder. "I'm so sorry," she said to no one in particular, and, wincing, picked her way back across the street. The others, too, drifted away, the couple arguing about whose idea it had been to bring the toddler out in the first place.

Al and Nishu turned back to whatever the thing was. It had re-placed the eye on its face and was picking dead leaves from its ear with a fingernail like the blade of a butter knife. It was extraordinary. It was totally naked, for one thing, and Al realized now he had kicked it right where its dick would have been, if it had a dick. Its skin was brown and gray and knobby and knotty. It didn't even come up to Al's waist. Its skinny legs bent backward at the knees. Its four arms sprang from one another like branches. Here and there on its body grew patches of moss, and it was covered everywhere with mud. Through the mud coating its face, its teeth shone yellow. It was smiling. It was awful.

"What is it?" Al whispered.

"It's a troll," Nishu said. "Like in the stories. You're a troll, right?"

The troll grunted. "Some call me that," he said in a deep voice. The eye was as red as Al's uncle's, the one who did drugs. "You children are in trouble, I think." His voice sounded like a mournful wind. He sounded like he was sad about their problem and had been for thou-sands of years.

Al didn't think he was actually sad about it, though. "Yeah, some-thing's going on," he said.

The troll's eye focused on him. He flicked away the object he'd pulled from his ear, and it took wing in midair and buzzed away. "You want so much," the troll said to Al. "It's delectable."

"Let's go, Al, let's go," Nishu was muttering. "Come on."

"We're going to leave now," Al said to the troll. "Thanks for, um, for helping us."

"Going?" said the troll. "Helping?" He tilted his head as if to listen. The neighborhood was suddenly alert again, doors opening, lights turning on. In the distance the barefoot woman yelled "WHERE ARE THEY?"

"Fine! What do we do to make it stop?"

"It's good that you asked," said the troll, suddenly obsequious. He climbed onto the pipe and sat down, his weird chicken legs dangling in front of the opening. "I do want to help. You need only answer me three questions."

"Really," Al said.

"Are you kidding me?" Nishu said.

"Three questions?"

"Come on."

"Silence!" the troll snapped. "You must answer these questions three or your life will be an everlasting torment!"

"Okay, okay," they said.

"I hope these aren't, like, Trivial Pursuit questions," Al added.

"I'm bad at those," Nishu said.

"You will have the answers," the troll said. A low, quiet rumbling filled the world. "You must only answer truthfully. Answer true, and I will release you from the curse you suffer. Attempt to deceive me, and I will know."

Al looked at Nishu, who shrugged. This was so cheesy. He didn't even like fantasy stories. At his old school, a kid had taken everyone to *The NeverEnding Story* for his birthday party, and he'd thought it was totally stupid. Princesses and flying dogs and made-up creatures. And now here he was, arguing with a made-up creature on a lawn in some misbegotten part of Milwaukee. He tried to remember anything about the old fairy tales, but all he could recall was that if you answered the questions you got to cross the bridge—"Where's your bridge?" he asked. "Aren't trolls supposed to be guarding bridges?"

The troll straightened up, wounded. "That's a myth," he said.

"You're a myth," Nishu pointed out.

"Not all trolls have bridges!"

"Is it, like, the bigger trolls get the bridges?" Al asked. "That happens to me. I get picked last even though—"

"Silence!" In one motion the troll slid down the side of the pipe and pulled the eye off its face. He stepped toward Al, holding the horrible eye out, and Al felt a shudder work its way through his body. The eye was doing something terrible to his insides. He fell down, shaking, and heard Nishu calling, "Stop it, stop it!"

He returned to himself. The sidewalk was cold. Nishu was crying. "Just ask your questions! We'll answer them!" he said.

"I ask this first," the troll said, scowling down at Al. Al registered, somewhere beyond the lingering pain and fear, how proud and scornful the troll was, how much he'd hated being made fun of. "Who is the person you have hurt the most?"

"Why do you want to know that?" Al said. He felt like he'd been emptied out and then everything had been put back in the wrong place.

"It is my payment," the troll said. "It is what I require."

Al already felt miserable, so he said, "I'll tell you." What did it matter if he felt worse? Trying to control the trembling in his voice, he told the troll about the day he called Amy Friedman ugly in front of the entire class, because he wanted the popular kids to laugh at the joke. Amy, who had been nice to him since the day he'd arrived, who'd come over to his house and watched cartoons, who'd shared her Fruit Roll-Ups with him. Even as he told the story, he felt the troll reaching for him, fondling the story inside his memory, plucking at its worst threads and delighting in the music they made. Al now recalled, with exquisite clarity, the look of anger on Amy's face, mixed with disappointment. He'd gotten the laugh he'd hoped for from boys like Aaron Sheahan and Jim Lynch, but had barely heard it, because his shame and regret were instant and total.

It happened during a group project in social studies class, while Mr. Brock was out of the room. Amy immediately got up and took the bathroom pass, and Al remained at his desk, listening to Aaron and Jim repeat the joke a few times before they got bored and returned to making fun of him.

The troll seemed to hold the memory in his hand, inspecting it with a connoisseur's eye. "It will do," he said. He turned to Nishu. "And you?"

Nishu was staring at the ground. He muttered something about his grandma.

"My ears aren't what they used to be, boy," said the troll, gesturing toward his quite outrageously large ears. "Speak up."

"Does he have to say it out loud?" Al said. "You're already in our brains. Just take it."

"He must say it. That is how it becomes mine."

Nishu said, a little louder, "It's my fault my grandma died."

The troll lit up. "Go on."

"She was visiting us," Nishu said. "We were at Winkie's, and she got lost. And she was calling for me, and there were these high schoolers there, and they were making fun of her. 'Nishu, Nishu.' 'Go back to India.'" Tears streaked his cheeks. Al tried not to look, to give him privacy. But the story he was telling was a foreswearing of the private.

It was the worst of him, like Al's story was the worst of Al, displayed in the open air. "And I hid. I was a coward and I hid behind the birthday cards. I didn't say anything."

"You were afraid," the troll said. "Why?"

"I didn't want them to tease me," Nishu said.

"And what happened?"

Nishu whispered, "The guys kept bothering her, and she got more and more upset, and she fell in the store, and the next day she died." His hands were in his pockets. He seemed to be unwilling to wipe his tears.

The troll opened his arms wide. Al's memory was flooded with new detail. He recalled that when Amy returned to the classroom she went straight to Mr. Brock. No punishment was necessary, he wanted to say from his seat. He already felt terrible. But all that happened after their quiet conversation was that Amy was moved to a different table for the group project. She sat with girlfriends for lunch, carefully placing herself in the middle of all of them. Al tried to sit with Aaron and Jim but they told him the seats were saved. He took his lunch to the library and ate there, alone.

And it made it worse to know that the troll had this memory, too, and that it delighted him. It might have offered Al some relief to confess the story to a friend, to receive absolution from someone he cared about. For this repulsive creature to enjoy it so made him even more ashamed. He saw Nishu with his hands over his face and knew the troll had done the same thing to him. The troll smiled his toothy smile. "My gift to you in return."

He clambered back up onto the pipe. "Now, the second question," the troll said. "What is your happiest memory?"

Al looked up. "No way," he said.

Underneath them the ground trembled once again, and the troll's eye seemed to glow with the fire of the earth. "You are mistaken," he said, his voice an earthquake's rumble. "You do not have a choice. When you arrived here with your hearts full of want, you called me. And once I am called, I *will have* my tribute."

"I'll tell it," Nishu said. He seemed eager to move his mind from the terrible topic of his grandmother. "My happiest memory is when I won the spelling bee," he said. "Is that what you're talking about?" The troll simply stared at him with a look of hunger. "Okaayyyy . . . Just, it was in September. And everyone already thought I was a nerd, so who cared, I studied really hard and beat all the eighth graders. I spelled *ecru* to win. That's a color, and I knew it because it was on a list of spelling bee words my teacher gave me. I got a trophy and they said my name on morning announcements."

The troll smiled. Nishu said, "Is that . . ." but then faltered into silence. The troll's bulging eye turned toward Al. The creature had accepted Nishu's story with a kind of perverted delight. Al could think of any number of wonderful memories he had no interest in sharing with this creepazoid.

"My happiest memory," he said. He laughed nervously. "Gotta be when my mom and I went to Wisconsin Dells. We went to a water park with huge slides, and there was one that was, like, going off a *cliff*, it's so steep. You lie on your stomach and it's like"—he traced the arc of the slide in the air with his hand—"*shoooom*. It was so awesome."

The troll looked at him for a moment. In the distance, dogs howled. Then the troll pointed the eye at Nishu, who fell over, crying out and clutching his stomach.

"No!" protested Al. "I really did that! I really went there!"

The troll's blind face turned toward him even as the eye watched Nishu writhing on the ground. The space where his eye belonged was dark and bottomless. "*Lies*," he hissed.

"Stop!" Al said. "Okay! I'll tell you!"

Nishu fell still. The troll replaced the eye. Al pulled Nishu to his feet but couldn't look him in the face. He was ashamed at what his self-ishness had caused.

"I met a girl," he finally said. "My mom sent me to College for Kids at UWM. We ate lunch together and we talked and she really liked me. And for the rest of the week, we were boyfriend and girlfriend. And she"—he felt so stupid, blushing in front of this leering monster—"she kissed me. We were in the dorm lounge, we got to stay in the dorms, and she kissed me."

"Jeez, your memory is a lot cooler than mine," Nishu said.

"There's something more," the troll insisted.

"We didn't do anything more!"

"Not your pawings," the troll said. "There was something she did that made you love her."

Al turned away. How did he know that?

"You will tell me," the troll said in a flat voice.

"That first day," Al said quietly. "After we ate lunch. She told me her phone number in the dorms. But so I wouldn't forget it she took my hand and . . ." He still remembered the feeling of Dana's finger on his palm, the way she looked up at him after. He'd never had someone show him, in such a simple way, that she liked him.

"Yes?"

"She typed the number on my hand." He held his own hand out and pressed his palm like the buttons of a telephone, five digits for her dorm room's number: four, three, eight, five.

"Yes," the troll breathed. "Yes, that's it."

The eye was in the troll's hand again, blinking rapidly. Al himself was holding out his own hand but had no idea why. He'd been thinking of Dana, of something that was important to him, but when he tried now to remember what it was, his mind shied away like a hand from something hot.

Nishu was gaping at the troll. "Give it back," Nishu said.

"They are mine," the troll said.

"Nishu, I remember yours," Al said, "you won the spelling bee. You spelled some word, some color." Nishu nodded, eyes wide. Yes, yes, yes. "And they gave you a trophy." But as soon as he stopped talking, Nishu's face fell.

"I can't remember," Nishu said miserably. And Al couldn't remember what it was about Dana that made her matter. Did she even matter? She must. Why would he remember her name otherwise? Had she liked him?

Around them the night was still and dark. They were alone on a corner far from home, facing a creature who had taken something important from each of them, and wanted even more. Nishu took off his backpack, dropped it on the ground, and sat down next to it.

"My final question," the troll said. "What is your most valued possession?"

Al looked away. The troll already knew what it was, he was certain.

"My rabbit's foot," Nishu said.

"The *Playboy* I found," Al said.

Nishu looked at Al in plain astonishment. "No way," he said. Then: "No!" For in one hand the troll held the *Playboy*, and in another a brown rabbit's foot. The troll cackled, and something about seeing those muddy hands despoiling the one beautiful thing he owned made Al snap. He ran at the troll, shouting, but the troll neatly sidestepped him and danced toward the culvert. In a moment he had disappeared into the dark mouth of the pipe. They could hear his laughter echoing off the steel.

Here was what Nishu had remembered when the troll had spread his arms. That before the boys had started taunting his grandmother, he'd argued with her because he wanted a rabbit's foot that was on sale at the counter. She told him she'd rather buy him something he could really use, and he'd stomped off. What a baby he'd been! It all came flooding back.

And he remembered that after the boys had finally left his grandmother alone, she'd continued calling for him, "Nishu! Nishu!" And then he'd heard her fall, and even then, he'd stayed frozen behind the birthday cards, until he heard a store employee rushing over, saying, "Ma'am? Ma'am?" And finally he'd come out around the display and seen her sitting on the floor, trying to wave away the clerks gathered around her, and the way her face lit up when she saw him! Like he was her eight-year-old hero, coming to her rescue. "Nishu beta," she said. "I knew you'd come." And she held out a paper bag to him, and in the paper bag was the stupid rabbit's foot. She'd bought it after all. She was so happy to give it to him. She loved him so much. She reached out her hand to touch his face, and her eyes were full of adoration.

It was those eyes Nishu thought of now, as he clambered into the ditch at the pipe's entrance. "We have to go after him," he said.

Al followed him, a determined look on his face. "I gotta get my magazine back," he said.

"Plus our memories."

"Right, those too," Al said. "I just wish we had a flashlight." Nishu pulled his keychain from his backpack and turned on the tiny flashlight, shining it into Al's face. "Oh, sweet!"

The light's beam was narrow but bright. He shined it into the pipe: rusted, corrugated walls; a trickle of dirty water and ice along the floor. They had to crouch a little to walk through, but it was roomier inside than Nishu would have guessed. Their boots thumped thickly against the steel. After just a few steps it was entirely dark, with only the flashlight stabbing through the black. Behind them, a circle of street light receded into the distance.

"It smells bad," Al said. "Do you think he's waiting for us?"

"Maybe we'll corner him," Nishu said.

"Or maybe he's waiting for us."

"It's just like a movie," said Nishu. He put on an announcer's voice, which echoed in the pipe. "The hero enters a dark cave. He sees the face of evil—and sees that it shares his own face."

"That's cool," said Al. "Is that from some kind of Indian movie?"

"It's *The Empire Strikes Back*."

"Right. Sorry."

Up ahead, something glinted in the flashlight's beam. Al made a noise and hurried forward. He picked up the glossy paper and held it up solemnly: an Absolut Vodka ad, the back cover of his *Playboy*. Nishu took it and, with great ceremony, placed it in his backpack.

On the wall near where the page had fallen, a line was cut through the corrugated steel. Nishu traced the line with his light, marking a circle about the size of a garbage can lid. "He must have gone through there, right?" He shoved at the steel, but it didn't budge. There was no handle or anything. He tried to hook his fingers into the crack, but only bent a fingernail.

"There's gotta be a magic password," he said. "Like 'speak friend and enter.' That's how these always work."

"Open sesame!" Al said.

"I don't think that's it."

"Well, you try something, then."

Nishu stood up as straight as he could, stared directly at the door, took a deep breath, and said, "*Mellon!*"

"Melon?"

"*Mellon*," Nishu said. "It means *friend* in Elvish."

Al clearly had no idea what Nishu was talking about, and said, "Abracadabra!"

"Do you know any other languages?"

"Nope."

"Open, please!" said Nishu.

"Will you please open?"

"Wait, I've got it. Password!"

"Trolls suck!"

Nishu played the flashlight along the top of the circle. "There's something scratched in here. Must be trollish."

"Stupid troll. Probably it's like, 'ugh ugh gug ugh.'" They both danced around emitting grunts. Nothing happened, but now they were having a good time. "It's too bad whatsisname isn't here, with his fart tape," Al said. "Probably if we played the exact right fart, this thing would open up."

Nishu blew a raspberry. Al made some fart noises with his hands. "I can do a great fart with my armpit, but it's too cold," Nishu complained.

"The password is . . . shit."

"Asshole!"

"Shitface!"

"Fuckface!"

"Fucker!"

"Fucking . . . fuckity fuck!"

They were both giggling now. Nishu, hands on knees, said, "I got it! *Balls*."

"Wiener!"

"Ballsack!"

Al clasped his hands together, as if praying. "Please let us in, Mr. Troll. The password is 'hairy nuts.'"

Al was doubled over. Nishu was laughing so hard he could hardly breathe. And suddenly with a crunching sound the circular door opened, and they both absolutely lost it at the idea that the password *was* "hairy nuts," both of them positively wheezing with laughter, but then Nishu felt something inside his chest, a hand pulling at his lungs, and he stopped laughing—the laughter was drawn out of him some-how. He could almost *see* it, a smudge in the air departing his body and floating up into the scratches on the wall. It was happening to Al, too, who was still bent over but clutched at his throat, his eyes wide.

They were silent. Nishu pulled the door the rest of the way open, revealing a dark, dripping hole. Nishu couldn't imagine what was so funny about those childish words they'd been shouting. He couldn't imagine what was funny at all.

"That's something else he took away from us," Al said.

This passageway was narrower than the pipe—small enough that even Al, not that tall himself, had to watch out for the ceiling. Nishu's sleeves and pant legs were getting muddier and muddier. His mom was going to give him a whole lecture. Or maybe she would hug him, sim-ply glad he was safe? She was often a mystery to him. He found himself thinking of her, and this tunnel, and the troll they sought. He thought of the water that trickled down the tunnel and froze, the water that would in spring thaw and flow riverward and then lakeward and then through the Great Lakes into the ocean. The water had been flowing forever, long before the troll or whoever had dug this tunnel, had crept through cracks and fractures, battling its way to where it wanted to be.

A drop plopped onto his cheek. He wiped it off. A millipede scur-ried ahead of his boot.

That water didn't worry about what would happen to it. It charged forward, it burrowed through rock and stone. Nishu couldn't bring his grandmother back, but he could follow this path wherever it went, and he could fight this stupid troll when he got to the end of it. He could get back his memory, whatever it was. "Hey," he said. "What was my happy memory?"

"You won the spelling bee."

"God, really? What a nerdy memory. Yours was about kissing a girl!"

"Oh, wow," Al said. "I gotta get that back."

Nishu thought about how this tunnel was just a tiny part of the enormous world that existed underground, the caves and rivers and the tunnels and sewers of humans. And all of it was invisible to him, every day—all of it was concealed from the aboveground world; yet if this tunnel was evidence, it was inhabited by creatures innumerable, large and small.

It was how he felt, in his real life, about his mother and his father and the long life they'd lived in India, before he was born—the stories he never wanted to hear. Their life now, in this American suburb, rested upon layers of history: their childhoods in Bombay, their years of school, the flight his dad took to America. Why were they in Milwaukee? He didn't have any idea. Hell, there had been who knows how many years before he'd even been born! It made everything they did so inexplicable. How could they, for example, argue so often, and yet still, once in a while, finish each other's sentences and laugh in unison?

What else was not visible to him? What else could he not see? Al, for example. He knew nothing about this kid. He was responsible, in some way, for what had happened to them up there. But he trusted him now. But did he understand him? Did he understand anyone?

As they crept farther, the smell Nishu had first noticed in the pipe grew stronger. It was rank and burnt. And Nishu was pretty sure the passage was getting warmer. In fact, under his coat, he was sweating.

The tunnel descended three, four, five steps, and then they were in some larger chamber, their footsteps reverberating off the walls. The smell was overpowering here. Nishu covered his face with one hand, using the other to point the flashlight around, picking out details on the opposite wall, as far away as first base was from second. Someone had carved a row of tall spikes into the wall. He realized that there was some natural light here, a hint of reddish-orange, flickering as if from a torch. And a low, rhythmic *whoosh*. Trucks on a highway, or—"Oh," Nishu said, overcome by a dreadful feeling, because the spikes moved slightly, and the wall was not a wall but fur, and the fur rippled gently because it belonged to something big.

Nishu switched off the flashlight. Al grabbed his arm. For a moment they stood paralyzed in the dark, as the sound—they realized, now, it was breathing—stopped. The chamber was filled with a terrible anticipatory silence, the quiet before a terrible thing happened.

A terrible thing didn't happen. In the dark, the creature settled into a new position. It seemed to take up so much of this chamber, so much more than any animal should. The reddish light, Nishu saw, was leaking from behind two enormous sets of sleeping eyelids. When the thing began breathing again, even and slow, Al took his hand off Nishu's arm.

Nishu had never considered if there was a whisper quieter than his regular whisper. It turned out he had a whole nother register of whisper available to him, something subvocal, a whisper that never left his throat. In that whisper, he and Al worked out that there was an exit to their right, they could see a glow coming from it, and they could reach it without going near the monster, whatever it was. They moved carefully, right hands on the warm, damp wall for balance, Nishu shielding the flashlight with his hand so it cast only the palest glow on the floor.

When they reached the exit and found themselves in another passage, Al emitted a moan. Nishu shushed him.

The tunnel here was illuminated, somehow, by glowing jewels embedded in the wall. Nishu could see Al looking at them curiously, considering whether to pry one out, and he said, "No. It's a trap." Al brought his hand to his throat, coughed uncomfortably, and nodded.

In science class, Nishu had seen what diamonds look like when they come out of a mine, and they just looked like rocks, not like these gaudy crystals glowing as if they had light bulbs inside them.

As they walked, the smell of the monster faded, but the smell of the earth itself was becoming overpowering. After one more turn Nishu stopped short and Al walked straight into his back. They stood at the threshold of a small, bizarre room, in the middle of which sat a small, bizarre chair, on top of which sat the troll.

The room. Later, they would try to remember what the room looked like. He and Al, attempting to reconstruct their trip underground, even tried to draw a diagram of it. But sitting in Nishu's rec room, they found their memories stymied, because the room was every shape but no shape, expansive but claustrophobic, ornately decorated but dirty and decrepit. It was perfectly round but also had corners. In those corners skulked small things with many legs. Light came from nowhere, light came from the rock walls themselves, which pulsed like a heart. Light came from the constellations of jewels stitched into the ceiling. Light came from the chair.

The chair. The chair was living earth, crumbling dirt and wet mud and roots and chunks of ice. Through the chair squirmed worms and insects, all of them scurrying hectically as bugs do when you turn over a rock. They wove into and out of the earthen chair, which was shaped like a bowl. The outside of the bowl was wreathed with tiny blue flowers, which swayed and writhed as if alive, responding to the creatures wriggling in their roots. Inside the bowl sat the troll.

The troll. His legs were crossed like a kindergartner's. His smile was bright with triumph. It was instantly, terribly clear that he'd expected them, was waiting for them, and that by arriving in his lair they'd given him exactly what he wanted. Hovering over one of his hands was a disturbance in the air, a smear, which Nishu thought must be the laughs that had been taken from them in the pipe. And in another hand was the troll's eye, rolling ecstatically. The troll opened his disgusting mouth and laughed. He looked ready to give a whole gloating speech.

"What a journey you've—gaaaa!!"

For Nishu heard himself shout and felt himself charge forward, backpack held in front, and he plowed into the troll and his chair at full speed. The earthen structure collapsed instantly, flowers scattering everywhere, and Nishu pinned the troll in the mud. The troll's spindly arms were battering his shoulders, but Nishu grabbed the creature's knobby, eyeless head and shoved it into his backpack. The eye—where was the eye? "There!" Nishu called to Al, pointing into the dirt where the eye had fallen and where one troll hand was scrabbling for it. Al rushed over and kicked the eyeball into one of the room's infinite corners, where it scattered the chittering creatures as it bounced into the wall.

Nishu had gotten the grunting, wiggling troll's torso into the backpack, which was very roomy. He could fit most of his violin case in there. Al pushed on the troll's dirty, kicking legs and mushroomy feet, finally squashing them down far enough that Nishu could wrench the zipper closed. Then they both danced away from the collapsed throne, brushing bugs and worms from their clothes and pants. Nishu screamed when he saw a millipede the length of a hot dog crawling up Al's back, but he reached to brush it off. Al screamed when Nishu touched his neck, screamed again when he saw the millipede land on the floor and burrow into the earth.

They stood there, staring at each other, dumbfounded. The ground rumbled. A groan belched forth from the earth's depths. A spurt of dirty water bubbled up underneath the mud pile. Inside the bag, the troll screamed curses. Nishu took the backpack by the straps, held it as high as he could, then dropped it onto the ground. There was a thud, then silence.

Al laughed. Then he said, "Hey!"

"I felt mine come back, too," said Nishu. "Not the memory, though."

Al and Nishu turned together to the eye, which sat against the wall, peering at them. Al stepped toward it gingerly. They both remembered what that eye had done to them. But out of the troll's hands, it seemed to have no power. Al, making a face, poked the eyeball with a finger.

"Gross," said Nishu.

"It's not *that* bad," Al said. He picked it up and handed it to Nishu. It was about the size and weight of a softball. The surface was slick, gritty where it was covered in dirt, but not slimy or anything. He avoided touching the iris and pupil. Al pointed at the backpack. "Will he be able to break out of there?"

"It's waterproof," Nishu said.

"I *will* break out," said the muffled voice of the troll. "And when I do—"

"Hey, what's your name?" Al asked.

The troll was shocked briefly into silence. Then: "*My* name?"

"Yeah. You're a troll or a gnome or whatever. Do you have a name we should call you?"

"You will not distract me from my purpose," the troll said, and the bag bulged where he threw his elbow.

"Okay, whatever," Al said. "We'll just call you Shitface, if that's what you want." Nishu hid a laugh behind his hand.

The troll sounded wounded. "My name is known only to me. I will not reveal it."

"Okay, Shitface. Enjoy being in a backpack."

"I live underground," the troll snapped. "This is nothing to me. I am quite comfortable." Perhaps this was true, although he was still upside down and his feet were still kicking at the top.

"I'm holding your eye," Nishu said. "Seems like a fun toy." He tossed the eye in the air, experimentally, and caught it.

Al said, "Whoa there!"

"What are you doing with that?" the troll demanded. "Give it back!"

"I wonder how far you could throw that," Al said. Nishu underhanded it over to him, and Al fumbled the catch. The eye landed in the dirt with a wet thunk and rolled back toward Nishu. "Oops."

The backpack tipped over, the troll was kicking so hard. "Put that down this instant!"

"What *is* your purpose?" Al asked. He leaned down toward the backpack. The troll stopped struggling. "Why do you want our memories so bad?"

"Why do you want the food you eat?" the troll said. "It is the same. Your memories sustain me."

"But they're mine," Al said.

The troll chuckled. "Does the cow say such a thing to the farmer when he takes her milk?"

"Wow!" Nishu said. "Look at this!" He had brought the eye up to his face and discovered that he could see through it, look straight through the pupil from the back, and the world on the other side was a world transformed. The underground chamber was bright around him, bright as day. The backpack glowed dark from the inside. The destroyed chair was a throne of gold, the insects and worms glittering like jewels. The flowers strewn about the ground glowed blue and hot as a gas flame. He moved the eye away from his face and back: throne, mound of dirt; throne, mound of dirt.

He offered the eye to Al, who took it and held it up. "Whoa," Al agreed. "I can see *you*."

"What do I look like?"

"Like yourself. But there's more."

Nishu took the eye back and looked at Al and saw it. Standing before him was a boy in a jacket and jeans, a boy with pale skin and dark brown hair. But Nishu also saw the things Al wanted. His desperation to excel. His hunger to impress the rich kids, to become rich himself. His hope that his parents might get back together. These wants twirled around him, so vivid and bright Nishu thought he could touch them.

And he saw more. He saw Al's memory about the girl in his class, the one the troll had made worse, as if it were a creature perched upon the boy's shoulders. The creature changed from moment to moment, black to white to purple, changed from lizard to bird to person, almost a person, a grotesque caricature of Al himself. It shifted so quickly Nishu could never be quite sure what he saw. But every version whispered, unceasingly, in Al's ear.

"You saw this? About me?" There was so much there, so much more than he could have guessed. Al, nearly lost amid the chaos and swirl, nodded. "Well, I understand why he could trick us," Nishu said, dropping his hand to his side so the world looked regular again. "He could see everything."

"And now I see nothing," the troll said from inside the backpack. "What price do you demand for the return of my eye?"

"Why would we ever give it back to you?" Al asked.

"There's always a price."

Al looked at Nishu, who shrugged. It was true they couldn't leave the troll in there forever. Nishu's homework was in there, for example. And there were things the troll could give them.

"We want our memories back," Al said.

"And his *Playboy*," added Nishu.

"All our things. Reverse all the things you did to us."

Nishu nodded encouragingly. "And get us out of here."

"Get us out of here *safely*," Al said. "You can't use your magical eye powers to hurt us."

"Just, like, no loopholes, Shitface," Nishu said. "You can't find some loophole and then be like, 'Oh ha ha, there's a loophole.'"

"Fine," the troll said. "The deal is struck. I will lead you to where your treasures lie."

"And you'll fix our memories?"

"I'll need my eye."

Al considered. "Well, we'll do that once you get us out of here."

Nishu picked up the backpack with a grunt and hoisted it onto his back. "He's heavier than he looks," he told Al.

"I can take him when you get tired."

"Are you made of rocks?" Nishu asked the backpack.

"I am part mineral, yes."

"Ow! Stop kicking." An exasperated sound came from the bottom of the backpack. The troll was still upside down.

"Is there a way to get out where we don't have to go past the monster?"

"No," the troll said. "The hodag guards the only way out."

They both said, "A hodag!"

"A creature of fire and flesh," the troll said. "The spirit of an animal worked to death! Born from ashes and offal! An infernal punishment for man's corruption of a once-green world!"

"Sure," said Nishu. "Well, no alerting the hodag. You just gotta take us to where our things are."

"I shall," the troll said.

"'I shall,'" Al said. "What a freaking weirdo."

Nishu led the way out of the throne room, trudging up the pathway with the glowing gemstones. He could feel, now, that the path led very slightly upward, toward the street and then home. "Nishu," Al said, "hold still for a sec." He pointed at the backpack, where the troll's finger was creeping out of an eyelet like a vine, looking for a place to go. He slapped at it, and the finger retreated.

As they approached the dark room the monster slept in, Nishu turned on his flashlight. He was careful to train its beam away from the hodag. It was still and silent but for the creature's foul breaths.

"YOUR TREASURES ARE HERE," the troll called in a shrill voice.

"Shh!"

"JUST LOOK," the troll continued gleefully.

"Oh no," Al breathed. Nishu's flashlight had traveled across the opposite wall and reached a row of terrible shining claws. There, nestled in between the claws, was the rabbit's foot and the magazine. Susan smiled winningly from the cover.

"OH, DID THAT COUNT AS A LOOPHOLE?" the troll said, and that was when the hodag woke up.

The room filled instantly with a bloodred light as the great eyes opened. The monster grumbled and groaned, and flame and smoke flickered in the hodag's nose. And then the eyes focused on the boys, pinned to the opposite wall, and the beast roared. Even as the sound and the smell washed over them, they were running, ducking, banging their arms and heads on the muddy walls, frozen dirt raining all over them as they caromed down the tunnel. Nishu could hear the foul troll cackling inside the backpack; behind him, roars, crashing, the monster barreling into the wall at the tunnel entrance.

Nishu risked a look back and saw that the hodag was digging after them, its claws carving away chunks of the tunnel with each swipe. The troll was yelling, "Come, my child! Come and avenge me!" Nishu wished he had never trusted that asshole. He clocked his head on a root. Ahead of him Al suddenly tumbled from view, and before Nishu could stop himself he, too, had tripped out the circular door and landed inside the pipe with a clang. The eye flew out of Al's hand, rolled halfway up the side of the pipe, then rolled right back down. Al caught it on a bounce. Down the tunnel Nishu could see bright fire approaching, so he slammed the door shut. They sprinted back up the pipe, their breath coming in desperate puffs of steam.

When they got to the mouth of the pipe and clambered out, both boys collapsed on the freezing ground, panting. The air was so sharp and clean. The streetlights cast a comforting yellow glow. There was a single car on the street a block away, a bunch of normal houses, and no sign of the hodag.

"I think we lost him," Al wheezed.

"Why would you *say* that?" Nishu shouted, and then there was an eruption of mud and smoke and water across the street. A stop sign tipped over, clanging on the pavement. And there was the hodag, its eyes fire, its claws shining, its muscular body rippling under its fur. It shook like a dog, spraying dirt everywhere. Now they could see it was the size of a car. Ferocious teeth, a long spiked tail, horns like a bull's, smoke snorting from its nostrils. Water was spraying everywhere from some kind of broken pipe but the hodag didn't care. It focused on Nishu and Al across the street. It would be on them in no time at all. From inside the backpack the troll roared in triumph as the hodag took one step into the street, two steps, and that's when the van hit it.

The hodag spun away on impact, sparks flying from its horns as they scraped the pavement, and landed in a heap on the snow and ice piled up by the curb. The van screeched to a halt, glass from a headlight spangling the street. The window rolled down to reveal Sigmone behind the wheel. "Get in!" he yelled.

The hodag was grunting and struggling to its feet, steam whistling out of one ear. Al and Nishu ran to the back of the van and pulled the doors open. Inside, Joel and Mark and Ryan were piled against the front of the cabin, where they'd been thrown when Sigmone rammed the hodag. Joel was unzipping his bag, checking on his boom box.

"Where is Kevin?" Nishu cried, using both hands to throw in the backpack.

"We don't know," Mark said. "We think there's something weird about this neighborhood."

"Oh, no shit?" Al shouted, closing the doors behind him.

"Can I go?" Sigmone called from the front. "This monster thing is coming." The van shook. The hodag was at the passenger door.

"Go!" everyone shouted. Sigmone hit the gas. Instantly the back doors flew open and Al tumbled out.

"Shit!" everyone yelled. Sigmone stopped the van and they all fell into one another. When Nishu looked back out the wildly swinging doors, Al was lying in the street, hands over his head, while the hodag nosed at him. Nishu jumped out of the van, followed by the other boys, and ran toward Al. The beast glared at them, dipped its head, and took a few sideways shuffles. It didn't seem that scared by them. Why should it—none of them had claws or fangs or anything.

Something shattered next to the hodag and it jumped. Ryan was throwing ice chunks at it. "SOMETHING is WEIRD about this NEIGHBORHOOD," he shouted. Al grabbed a chunk from the pile at the curb and chucked it as hard as he could. The ice walloped the hodag right on the nose. It made a croaking sound, shook its head, and stepped away from Al, toward them.

Well, they had solved the immediate problem, but now there were other problems. Nishu looked to his left and saw Mark and Ryan. He looked to his right and saw Joel and a gigantic wolf, with claws and fangs. Nishu made a noise, and all the other boys looked and made a similar noise, except Joel, who just grinned like a madman.

The hodag stopped short. The wolf was bigger than him, almost as big as the van. The wolf took a step forward; the hodag stepped back, stepped back again, and then was splashing through the water, slithering into the hole it had made in the lawn.

Nishu ran to Al, who was now scrambling away from the wolf. "It's okay, it's Sigmone," Joel said. "He does that now." And indeed, the wolf was gone and there was Sigmone, shaking his head and walking back to the van.

Al's hands were scraped, but he otherwise seemed all right. Nishu helped him up. Al said, "Can we please just go to Burger King now?"

"Sigmone, you're really good at driving," Ryan said after they'd fully secured the door. "You're not old enough for your license though, right?"

"Dog years," Sigmone said.

Inside Nishu's backpack, the troll howled with fury. Its anguish seemed to boil and bubble from underneath them, from the pits of hell, a deep and clamorous bellow filling the van, echoing across epochs: the sound of an ageless creature desolate and defeated, the titanic despair of the broken earth summoned in one cacophonous roar.

"We caught a troll," Al said.

Joel held out his microphone. "Do you think he would do that again?"

BURGER KING

"This Burger King better not be freaking haunted," Mark said.

Ryan expressed concern about using the cash from the subscription envelopes to pay for dinner, but he was quickly outvoted. "The guy took us to the Monster Mash," Al said as they climbed out of the van.

"Then disappeared," Nishu said.

"No offense," Al said to Sigmone. "I mean, like, I'm not including you in—"

"RAAR!" Sigmone said, and Al quailed. Everyone cracked up. "I'm just messing with you," Sigmone said. "I'm a mean motherfucker from a distant land."

They stood in a circle in the parking lot, working out how much money they had. Nishu held up the backpack with both hands. "What are we going to do with this guy?"

He set the pack in the middle of the circle. From inside, the troll said, "I am willing to make a deal."

"We already made a deal with you!" Nishu said. "You cheated!"

All the way to the Burger King, Sigmone driving very cautiously, the other boys had held the troll's eye up to their faces and marveled at what it showed them. Now, as Al and Nishu argued with the creature in the backpack, Ryan held it up and looked at the Burger King. Through it, the restaurant looked like a palace. He could see the happy customers inside, eating their food; the employees and their plotting against the manager; the manager, who dreamed only of robbing the till and driving to Canada. He could also see the tormented souls of all the cows, circling the roof and lowing piteously, but he decided not to tell everyone else about that.

"We're going to open the bag," Nishu said, "and we'll give you your eye. And you're going to return all our things to us."

"I agree," the troll said.

"Or I'll eat you up in one bite," Sigmone said. "*Chomp chomp.* Like a appetizer before I get my Whopper."

"I agree," the troll repeated. Nishu unzipped the bag, just a little, and indicated to Ryan to slip the eye into it. The bag rustled, and then a knobby hand appeared, holding the rabbit's foot, muddy and squashed. Nishu took it without a word and slipped it into his pocket.

The hand reappeared, holding a mess of torn, burnt paper. "Nooo," Al said.

"Yo, was that a *Playboy*?" Joel asked. "Wow."

Al held the crumbling remains of his magazine. He tried flipping through it to find Susan and most of the pages fell onto the pavement and began blowing away. "Fix it!" he moaned.

"That is beyond my power," the troll said. The other boys observed a moment of respectful silence as Al walked over to the orange and brown trash can and slipped the magazine into its mouth.

"What about our memories?" Nishu said.

"I must gaze upon you in order to make those transformations," the troll said.

"Oh my God," Joel said, laughing. "Talk like a normal person."

"He sounds like he's trying to be Darth Vader," Ryan said.

Sigmone made obscene-phone-call breathing noises. "'I must gaze upon you,' come on."

Nishu unzipped the backpack and shook it upside down. The troll tumbled out and landed on his bony ass, followed by a cascade of notebooks and Nishu's science textbook, which thunked onto the troll's head. Everyone acknowledged how totally gross he looked. "No offense," Mark added.

The troll struggled to his feet and looked around at his tormentors. He shook his head, as if disappointed in himself. "It is done," he said finally. Al and Nishu felt their minds whole again: their best memories returned, their worst memories theirs alone.

The troll plucked the eye from its head and held it up like a shield. "You children," the troll said. "You think you have defeated me."

"Yeah, we defeated you," Nishu said.

"Nishu kicked your ass," Al said.

"He shoved you in a *backpack*," Ryan said. "That's pretty defeated."

From underneath the parking lot they heard a soft rumbling, like a truck three blocks away. "I saw you all," the troll said, his voice booming through the parking lot. "I saw your crimes, I saw your secret loves, I saw your fears. I brought the powers of Hampton Heights to bear to torment and punish. I, who has rested underneath Hampton Heights for generations, saw you intruders and saw the weakness in your hearts." From all the troll's fingers, from the lumpy skin of his back and shoulders, sprang bright green shoots. They bristled like a porcupine's quills, then grew blue flowers that trembled in the night air. "And I shall TAKE that weakness," he said, the eye moving wildly from boy to boy, "and it shall be the tool I use to DESTROY YOU ALL!"

"You look like a fuckin' Chia Pet," said Joel.

"Does this troll have a name?" Sigmone asked.

"We call him Shitface," Nishu said. Everyone lost it. The troll whirled around, the eye trying to focus on everyone at once. The flowers opened and closed like mouths. The rumbling faded, drowned out by their laughter.

"Shitface!"

"Perfect!"

"He even smells like it!"

"What's with the four arms?"

"Four arms!"

"Four fucking arms!"

Everyone was laughing now. The troll said, "That's simply the number of arms I have," and everyone laughed harder.

"Look at me, I'm a troll," Joel said, waving his arms around. "I got four arms!"

A car left the drive-thru and coasted past them. From a window, someone yelled, "Nice troll, assholes!"

The troll took a deep, long-suffering breath. The blue flowers had all wilted and he looked merely shaggy. He trudged away toward the dumpsters. At the edge of the parking lot he clambered over a mound of dirty snow and then was gone.

The boys walked toward the restaurant, still chuckling. Outside the door, a pair of high schoolers were smoking cigarettes and giving the eye to everyone who walked in. "What do you dudes want?" one said. He had the makings of a mustache and wore a trench coat over his Metallica shirt.

"We're here," Nishu said boldly, "to get the *cheeseburgers* we *deserve*."

The high schoolers looked at each other, cigarettes dangling from their mouths. "Hell yeah, man," the other one said. He opened the door for them, as grandly as a footman.

Inside it was warm and meaty. You could smell the smoke from the grill. Mark saw Heather Marchese standing at the register, looking bored as a coworker talked her ear off. He veered right, toward the bathrooms.

"What is it?" Ryan asked. "Hold on, guys." The group clustered around Mark.

"Nothing! Nothing." Mark shook his head. "It's just, there's a girl who works here. Don't look!" They all looked, at the exact moment Heather waved at Mark.

"Is she a *high schooler*?" said Nishu.

"You *know* her?" Al asked.

"Sort of," Mark said. "We go to church together."

"What's her name?" said Ryan.

"Heather."

The boys all repeated the name, reverently. Heather, who was in high school. Heather, who knew Mark well enough to wave at him.

"You should talk to her," Ryan said.

"I know, but what do I say?" Mark asked. "Will one of you go up there first?" The other boys shook their heads. No way.

Ryan was struck by the change in Mark. The confident salesman was gone. In his place, a nervous middle schooler. Ryan felt for him. It was hard to steel your courage to do something for someone you really liked.

"Come on," Ryan said to everyone. "We fought monsters and trolls and stuff tonight. We can figure out what to say to a girl."

"No way," said Sigmone.

"Look at me," said Ryan. They looked at him. "We are all going up there together, and we're all ordering our food together. Come on." He walked to the counter. Everyone followed him.

"Welcome to Burger King," the girl said. Ryan stepped up first. "Hi," he said. "We're celebrating."

"Oh yeah?" she said. "Celebrating what?"

"Surviving," Ryan said. Mark smiled at him, and he felt so much love he could hardly stand it. But it didn't hurt the way he thought it would.

The boys ordered ever-bigger dinners, exceeding one another's extravagances. A Whopper and fries became a Double Whopper and fries, plus onion rings, plus sodas, plus milkshakes for all. Finally,

Heather Marchese turned her beautiful face to Mark and said, with the hint of a smile, "And for you, sir?"

When Kevin saw the white van in the parking lot of the Burger King, he nearly wept with relief.

"Those parents are gonna kill you for sure," Theresa said as she pulled into the lot. She still seemed pretty angry, but that didn't matter, Kevin decided. She hadn't hung up when he called! She'd driven all the way out to this godforsaken neighborhood to help him! She still cared about him!

"As long as the kids are fine, the parents won't care," he said. "And I bet—oh, shit." She'd pulled up next to the van and they both saw the enormous scratches on its side, as if it had been attacked by several giant can openers.

"Oh my God."

"I told you! Monsters!"

"Are you gonna get fired?" she asked.

"No way," he said. "Richie drove his into the lake and he didn't even get suspended."

When Kevin had run to the corner by the tavern to discover that the van was gone, he'd been filled with dread, for sure. His dread had shifted into panic when a pack of wolves, each so big it seemed as though it should have its own dedicated habitat at the county zoo, burst from the underbrush and galloped across the street. A car screeched to a halt in the middle of Hampton, waited for the wolves to pass, and then just kept on going like it was nothing.

In the tavern, he gibbered into the pay phone: something about monsters, and skin, and the van, and wolves, and he didn't know where the kids were. Theresa had not sounded thrilled to hear from him, but blessedly she had agreed to drive out there and pick him up. "Don't drink any more," she said. "You've had enough."

As he waited in the entryway for her to arrive, he flinched every time he saw someone walk by on the sidewalk. Was that Laurie? Had she come after him? She hadn't seemed that happy with him, either, when he left. It was clear that whatever else he was, tonight he was a disappointment to women. And meanwhile, where were the kids? Where was the van? Was he going to be on the news tomorrow? He imagined Mike Gousha trying to pronounce "Kaczorowski" and was overcome by despair.

But you can't stay panicked forever. It took too much energy, and he was exhausted. By the time Theresa pulled up in her Honda, he'd calmed down enough to think, *I bet she wouldn't do this for Crazy TV Barry.*

The kids weren't on any of the blocks where he'd sent them to canvass. The streets were empty; one was blocked because of a water main break that was turning into a slushy lake on the street. Workers in orange vests pushed a stop sign upright, wading through the mess. They waved Theresa through.

"Wait a minute," he said. "What about Burger King?"

"Why would they even remember about Burger King?" she asked.

"Honestly, it's the main reason most of them come," he said. He'd hardly dared to hope, but there was the van, and there, through the window, were the kids, having a great time. They looked like an advertisement for Burger King. He was suddenly furious at them, for what they'd put him through. "Look at them, just laughing it up," he said. "Ow!"

She'd punched him in the arm. "Asshole!"

"What?"

"You left them on their own! While you got drunk!"

"I almost got killed!"

"Yeah, a monster. Kevin, I can smell her perfume. I hope you made her happy."

He thought back to the carnage in Laurie's bathroom. "No, I didn't," he said miserably. "I suppose Crazy TV Barry makes you happy."

"No," she said. "But he doesn't make me *un*happy. Sucks that that's what I'm willing to settle for."

"I'll call you!" he shouted after Theresa's car as she pulled away.

As he approached the restaurant he saw, again, the kids at their table. They were chattering happily, laughing, eating fries. Even the weird one with the fart tape seemed to be getting along with the others. A group of older kids were leaning up against a partition, talking to Sigmone. That guy was his most responsible paperboy—never missed a day, never got a complaint.

From out here in the dark, cold parking lot, the group in the Burger King looked as cozy as could be, a family gathered with joy around a communal table of burgers and shakes. He thought of Theresa, driving home now, no doubt even angrier at him than she was before. He thought of sitting with her at a table and smiling. He vowed at that moment that he would win her back, that he would become the kind of man she might admire. For now, he took a deep breath and walked to the door.

Two dirtbags smoking cigarettes looked Kevin up and down. "Hold up, hold up," one of them said, stepping in front of the door. "You wish to see the king?"

Kevin stopped short. "I want to go into Burger King, yes."

"We are the guardians of the throne, the mages of the clouds," the other dirtbag said. "If you wish to see the king, you must prove your valor in a test of strength."

The two dirtbags threw their hands into the air. As if a switch had been flipped, snow began falling in soft, silent flakes.

Kevin buried his head in his hands.

Sigmone had noticed faces he recognized at a booth by the window. The three people there had nearly finished eating and were talking avidly, their trays smeared with ketchup, their cups empty. As Sigmone approached, they turned to him. "Hey, man," Greg said.

"Hey!" Sigmone said. He didn't care that he seemed overenthusiastic. He couldn't believe they were here.

"You said you were going to Burger King," Justin said.

"We took a chance," Jenny said. She held out her carton with its last few fries. "Want to finish these?"

"I got my own," Sigmone said.

Joel showed up, carrying a tray laden with burgers. "Oh, hey guys," he said. "It's cool that you came here."

"Yeah, we're pretty cool," Justin said.

"We're gonna sit over here," Joel said, sliding the tray onto the table next door. After all that had happened, Sigmone couldn't quite bring himself to be embarrassed about Joel, not even when Joel started telling Ryan and Mark about how he'd spent the night with a hot older lady, and he could tell she'd wanted to make out, but he was a gentleman.

"How many subscriptions did you all actually sell?" Jenny asked everyone.

"We did okay," Al said. "We sold fifteen."

The other boys exploded in derision. "Fifteen!"

"What the hell!"

"Y'all were cheating!"

"Fifteen!"

Their laughter filled the restaurant. Al looked guilty. "Well, how many did you get?"

"Two!" said Mark.

"One!" said Joel. "Did you just write random addresses down?"

"Only at first," Al said, "but then things got weird."

Everyone continued laughing but did agree that things, indeed, had gotten weird.

The conversation fragmented around the table then. Al and Nishu talked about Al's Snow Service, which was going to need a second staff member soon. Sigmone and the high schoolers made plans for them to drive him out to Hampton Heights the next weekend. He could hang out with them and maybe even check in with his grandpa. And Joel, Ryan, and Mark talked to Heather, who'd persuaded her stupid manager to let her take a break. Ryan and Mark kept having to steer Joel away from enthusiastically explaining the fart tape.

"Hey, check it out, it's snowing," said Heather.

"Sigmone, can you drive in the snow?" Al asked.

"No problem," Sigmone said.

"Whoa," Joel said, pointing out the window into the parking lot. "Is that Kevin?"

They crowded around the booth, still messy with trays, faces pressed to the glass. In the parking lot, Kevin, stripped down to a T-shirt, circled one of the teenagers from the door, their gazes locked on each other. Kevin held the big knife from the front seat of the van. The teenager held a crooked staff before him like a spear. They were surrounded by a circle of dirtbags, all chanting in unison. The teenager facing Kevin raised his arms like a band conductor, the staff crackled with electricity, and wind swirled around them both, snow flying sideways into Kevin's face. Kevin braced himself, saw the kids in the window, and held the knife aloft. His face was illuminated with surprise and awe as the blade came alive with yellow fire. The chanting grew louder. The snow whirled. The flames leapt into the air.

Inside the Burger King, everyone stood shoulder to shoulder at the window. One of them said, "I just want to know what happens next."

ABOUT THE AUTHOR

Dan Kois is a writer, editor, and podcaster at Slate, where his work has been nominated for two National Magazine Awards and two Writers Guild Awards. He's the author of *Vintage Contemporaries* as well as three nonfiction books, a frequent guest on Slate's *Culture Gabfest* podcast, and host of *The Martin Chronicles*, a podcast about Martin Amis. He lives with his family in Arlington, Virginia.

Don't Miss Dan Kois's Phenomenal Debut

"An elegant and tender exploration of friendship, the passage of time, and what we lose and gain in the process of becoming ourselves. Part elegiac, part mindful of what nostalgia can obscure about the past, Dan Kois's novel provides precise insight into the defining moments of youth and adulthood, and finds grace and abundant possibility in both."

–DANIELLE EVANS, author of *Before You Suffocate Your Own Fool Self* and *The Office of Historical Corrections*